WELCOME BACK, STACEY!

Other books by
Ann M. Martin

Rachel Parker, Kindergarten Show-off
Eleven Kids, One Summer
Ma and Pa Dracula
Yours Turly, Shirley
Ten Kids, No Pets
Slam Book
Just a Summer Romance
Missing Since Monday
With You and Without You
Me and Katie (the Pest)
Stage Fright
Inside Out
Bummer Summer

BABY-SITTERS LITTLE SISTER series
THE BABY-SITTERS CLUB mysteries
THE BABY-SITTERS CLUB series

WELCOME BACK, STACEY!

Ann M. Martin

AN
APPLE
PAPERBACK

SCHOLASTIC INC.
New York Toronto London Auckland Sydney

This book is for
Courtenay Robertson Martin,
a new fan of
The Baby-sitters Club

Cover art by Hodges Soileau

ISBN 0-590-67396-3

12 11 10 9 8 7 6 5 4 3 2 1   3   6 7 8 9/9 0 1/0

Printed in the U.S.A.   40

CHAPTER 1

"Stacey? Do you think that if dinosaurs were still alive, a stegosaurus could beat a brontosaurus in a fight?"

"What?" I replied. I hadn't quite heard Henry's question. I felt bad. A baby-sitter should always pay attention to her charges.

"Could a stegosaurus beat a brontosaurus in a fight? If they were alive today?" Henry waited patiently for my answer. He and his little sister Grace were making pictures on long rolls of shelf paper with fat pastels. Henry had just drawn what looked like a big city. I had a feeling that the next thing he was going to do was draw dinosaurs in the city — and that my answer would be important to him *and* to his picture.

"Well, could a stegosaurus beat a brontosaurus in dinosaur days?" I asked. Henry and Grace and I live really near the American Museum of Natural History in New York City, and Henry likes to visit the dinosaur exhibits.

Henry shrugged. "I don't know," he replied. "I guess it doesn't *really* matter. I'll just pretend a steg could beat a bronto." (Henry is on familiar terms with dinosaurs. Oh, excuse me. With dinos.)

Maybe I better stop here and introduce Henry and Grace and myself. I am Stacey McGill and I'm thirteen years old. Henry and Grace and I live on the Upper West Side of New York City. In fact, we live in the same building. I live on the 12th floor and the Walkers live on the 18th floor. Mr. and Mrs. Walker are artists, and Henry and Grace, who are five and three, are my two favorite baby-sitting charges.

Believe me, I do a *lot* of baby-sitting. Sometimes I'm amazed by all the things that have happened to me because of baby-sitting. For instance, I live in a large (okay, a huge) apartment building with plenty of little kids, but not many kids my age — and hardly anyone else who's interested in sitting. So I get a lot of jobs, have a lot of fun (especially with Henry and Grace), and earn a lot of money.

That's just the beginning, though. I've lived in New York City all my life except for one year. That year, my parents and I (I'm an only child) lived in a small town in Connecticut called Stoneybrook. My dad had been transferred there by the company he works for. We thought the move was going to be permanent, so I was desperate to make friends in Stoneybrook — and fast. Guess how baby-sitting helped me. I heard about this group of girls who were starting something called the Babysitters Club. They wanted to run a business sitting for families in the neighborhood — and they were looking for another member! So I joined. Instant friends. I'm still really close to most of the girls in the club, especially Claudia Kishi. She's my Connecticut best friend. (My New York best friend is Laine Cummings.) Then there're Dawn Schafer, Mary Anne Spier, and Kristy Thomas. They're good friends, too. Mallory Pike is a little young to be a close friend, and I don't know Jessi Ramsey too well yet (Mal and Jessi replaced me when Dad was transferred again, and we moved back to New York), but I still consider them friends.

Anyway, yes, that's right. After a year in Connecticut, Dad's stupid company transferred him right back to where he'd been. Don't get me wrong. I ♡ New York, just like the bumper stickers and the T-shirts say. I really do ♡ it. I ♡ the stores, especially Bloomingdale's, the theaters, the museums, the parks, the excitement. I even ♡ tourists, because they add to the excitement. But I didn't ♡ all the trauma and trouble of moving twice in just a little over a year.

Still, we did move, and when we got back to New York I was thirteen, not twelve, and we moved into this huge building with all these kids, and I've been sitting practically ever since. Things aren't the same without the Baby-sitters Club, even though I consider myself the New York branch of the BSC. But I wouldn't trade big-city life for anything.

I wouldn't trade sitting for the Walkers, either. I adore Henry and Grace. There's just something wonderful about them. It's not that they're well behaved (which they are). It's not that they're creative and can always be entertained with art projects. No, I think it's that they're such caring kids. They look out for each other, they stick up for their friends, and they try very hard never to hurt anybody's feelings.

So of course Henry was pleasant about my being in outer space the afternoon he asked his dinosaur question, and then about my not knowing the answer.

"How are you doing?" I asked Grace, looking at her picture.

Grace was bent over, concentrating hard. She was drawing slowly and carefully, her tongue sticking out of the corner of her mouth.

"Fine," she replied, straightening up. "Do you like my picture, Stacey? It's an elephant. And the elephant is in a bathtub, but there's no water in it. He's taking a nap. See? There's his pillow."

Henry giggled. "Give him a blanket," he said. "And show that he's dreaming about a bronto."

"How do I draw a dream?" wondered Grace. She pulled at her curly hair.

"Like this." Henry drew a "dream bubble" over the elephant's head. "Now put a bronto in there," he instructed his little sister.

"Oh!" said Grace. "Thank you, Henry."

I smiled. What terrific kids. In fact, the whole Walker family is terrific. Mr. Walker is an artist and Mrs. Walker illustrates children's books. They're both pretty well known. The reason I was sitting for Grace and Henry that Wednesday afternoon was that a showing of

Mr. Walker's work was going to open soon, and the Walkers had gone to the gallery to help supervise the hanging of some of his paintings. I guess another thing you should know about the Walkers is that they're black. There aren't too many black families in our building. You know what's funny, though? When I'm with the Walkers I don't think of them as *black*, just as *people*. I feel the same way when I'm with Jessi Ramsey, one of the new members of the BSC. I don't see her as black, just as an eleven-year-old baby-sitter who's Mallory Pike's best friend. I have never understood the big deal about black or white, Jewish or Christian, Irish or Polish or Chinese or Mexican or Italian or who knows what.

Anyway, boy was I having trouble concentrating that day. It's a good thing Henry and Grace are so easy to sit for. Earlier, I'd been off in Never-Neverland, thinking about my parents.

Here's the thing about Mom and Dad. They have not been getting along too well lately. It's just like when Laine Cummings and I were in fifth grade. We called ourselves best friends, but we were forever getting into fights. Then we would snap our heads around, or turn our backs on each other, and one of us would say, "I'm not talking to you."

The other would reply, "I don't care."

"Good."

"Good."

"So there."

"So there."

Then we would spend about two days pretending that other girls were our new best friends, and finally we'd give it all up and realize that *we* were our only best friends. When that happened, we'd start sneaking looks at each other in class. Then one of us would offer a smile, usually the one who had said, "I'm not talking to you." After that, at our first opportunity — in the girls' room or the cafeteria or someplace — we'd apologize and make up. Sometimes I felt that the fights had been worth it, because making up was so nice. Considering how much my parents had been fighting and arguing lately, I certainly hoped that they felt the same way about making up.

I don't like hearing my parents argue. Sometimes it's scary. Not because I'm afraid they'll hit each other or anything, but because I never know what's going to come out of their mouths. They hurt each other with words instead of with fists, which is almost as bad. You can't take back either a punch or an insult. You can *apologize*, but what's done is done, what's said is said, and some things are hard to forget.

Like the time my father called my mother a selfish spendthrift. I hated both of them then. I hated my mother for doing whatever she'd done to cause my father to call her a selfish spendthrift, and I hated my father for having called her one, whether she was or not.

I had felt very confused.

"Hello!" called Mrs. Walker's voice then. "We're ho-ome!"

Henry and Grace jumped up from their little table in a frenzy of excitement.

"Mommymommymommymommymommy!" cried Grace.

She and Henry grabbed their pictures and tore into the living room.

Such pandemonium. You'd think the Walkers had been gone for two months instead of less than two hours. But it was awfully nice to see a couple of smiling, nonangry parents greeted so enthusiastically by their kids.

"How did everything go?" asked Mr.

Walker. (Grace had wrapped herself around his left leg.)

"Oh, fine, as usual," I replied, grinning. "We have plenty of masterpieces to show you."

"Daddy, can we hang my dino-fight in your show?" asked Henry.

"We'll see," said Mr. Walker.

Mrs. Walker paid me then, and Henry and Grace each had to hug me twice before I could leave. When the door was closed behind me, I walked to the elevator and rode down to the 12th floor.

The doors opened.

I could hear the fight even before I reached my apartment.

Mom and Dad were at it again.

Slowly I crept toward 12E.

"Look at this bill!" my father was yelling, and I mean *yelling*. "Four hundred and ninety dollars on jewelry at Altman's? Do you think I'm made of money?"

"You ought to be," replied my mother sarcastically. "You practically live at the office. I'm surprised Stacey recognizes you anymore."

I looked at my watch. Five-thirty. What was

Dad doing at home? He usually didn't get home until seven-thirty or eight. Mom and I were used to eating our dinners alone those days.

I put my hand on the doorknob and felt around in my pocket for my keys. I was about to go inside. But then I drew back. I did not want to walk in on the middle of a fight. I did that once and my parents immediately started arguing about *me*. See, I have diabetes and I have to stay on a strict low-sugar diet, give myself insulin shots everyday, and go to the doctor a lot. If I don't do those things, I could get really sick. So Mom and Dad would argue over whether I'd stick to my diet at a party (of course I would), or whether I should be allowed to go to summer camp (they finally let me). That kind of thing.

No more noises were coming from inside my apartment, so I decided it would be safe to go inside. I was just about to put the key in the lock when my father positively roared, "Fifteen hundred and sixty-eight dollars at Tiffany's. Good lord, what did you *buy?*"

CHAPTER 2

I stood there, frozen. I couldn't move. Part of me was wondering just what my mother *had* bought, but most of me was waiting to hear how she'd answer Dad. Sometimes she cries.

Not that time. She spat out her answer as if the words tasted bad. "Jewelry," she said. "Maybe if you were home more often I wouldn't be so bored. When I get bored I shop . . . sometimes."

"*Some*times? Try all the time. And if you're so bored, get a job," shouted Dad. "Do something useful with your life instead of supporting every store in the city. Spend more time with your daughter."

"Stacey doesn't need me so much anymore," replied Mom. Now she did sound a little teary.

"Doesn't need you!? She's a diabetic."

"Exactly. She's a diabetic. Not an invalid. And she's thirteen. She's growing up. It would be nice, though, for her to see her father. I mean, just occasionally. So she doesn't forget what he looks like. I hope she's going to . . . afterward." (What had Mom said? I'd missed something.) She was sounding sarcastic again, though, not tearful.

(And how had I gotten into this argument, anyway?)

"Do you know what you are?" my mother continued. (Her voice was as loud as my father's. I hoped our neighbors were enjoying the fight.) "You're a workaholic," she screamed.

"I have to be, to pay all your bills," retorted Dad. "Besides, you always ask too much of me. You expect . . . six different places at once." (I was missing words again.) "At the office, with you, with Stacey, with our friends. You've been too darn demanding. And you're a spoiled brat. You even expect us to move out of the city. Well, soon we won't have to worry about any of those things."

They wouldn't? Why not? I wondered.

"Moving would be healthier for Stacey. She was in much better shape when we lived in Connecticut."

"So move," said Dad. "But I'm not going to commute on top of everything else. And what are you going to do without Tiffany's?"

"Find another jewelry store," snapped my mother. "I've *got* to . . ."

(Darn. What was I missing? I pressed my ear to the door.)

"Well," said my father, "Stacey and I are perfectly happy."

I was trembling. I'd heard my parents fight before, but not like this. They'd fought about a restaurant bill being too high, or about Dad getting home from work later than usual three nights in a row, but I'd never heard anything like this. It sounded much worse. I was scared to death. Mom wanted to leave the city? Dad thought Mom was lazy and demanding and spent all his money the wrong way? (I thought it was *their* money.)

Slowly I stepped back. I pulled my keys away from the lock. I dropped them in my pocket. Then I crept down the hall (as if there were a chance my parents could hear me over their shouting). I sped up when I reached 12C and ran the last few yards to the elevator. I poked frantically at the down button. A few seconds later, the elevator arrived with a crash. The doors opened up, allowed me inside, and closed.

ZOOM.

Our elevator never travels naturally. It clanks and swooshes and comes to stomach-dropping stops.

The doors opened in the lobby. I ignored Lloyd and Isaac on duty at the desk, and even James as he held the front door open for me. I just ran. I ran by them, out onto the sidewalk, and all the way to my friend Laine Cummings' apartment, which is several blocks away. By the time I reached it, I was crying.

Laine lives in one of the fanciest apartment buildings in all of New York City. It's called the Dakota. Lots of famous people have lived there, and still do, and I *think* the movie *Rosemary's Baby* was filmed in it. Mr. Cummings is a big-time producer of Broadway plays, and Laine's family has buckets of money.

Naturally, with so many famous people and so much wealth, the security at the Dakota Apartments is pretty tight. But the guards know me, since Laine and I have been friends for years, so I never have any trouble getting in. Not even on that day when I was crying, and my face was flushed and my hair a mess from all that running.

When I reached the door to the Cummingses' apartment, Laine opened it, gawked at me for a second, and led me through the living room, down a hallway, and into her bedroom.

She closed her door behind us. "What on earth is wrong?" she asked.

I couldn't blame her for looking so surprised. After all, I'd been fine in school that day. (Laine and I go to the same private school.)

"You aren't sick again, are you?" she asked worriedly.

I shook my head. Then I tried to calm down. I knew that if I spoke, my voice would wobble, so I took a few deep breaths. At last I managed to say, "I came home from baby-sitting and Mom and Dad were fighting."

"Your father's home already?" asked Laine.

I nodded. "I don't know when he got there. I didn't even go inside my apartment. I just stood at the door and listened. I could hear almost every word. They were really going at it." For some reason, as soon as I said that, I knew I was going to cry. And I did. In a major, awful, hiccuping, gulping way.

Laine, who had been kneeling on the floor, moved to the bed and sat down next to me.

She put an arm across my shoulder. "What were they fighting about?" she asked after a few moments.

"Oh," I said, wiping my eyes, "everything. Everything in their lives. Money, New York, me."

"You?"

I nodded again. "I think I was just an excuse, though. Dad said Mom should spend less time shopping and more time with me. But I don't feel, like, neglected or anything. And Mom said she wants to move out of the city because it would be healthier for me, but I don't want to move out of the city."

"Move out of the city to where?" asked Laine.

"I don't know. I guess to Long Island or someplace nearby."

"Oh."

I looked at Laine. Over the years we've been through good times and bad times. And we're both pretty sophisticated, having grown up in the city and all, but of the two of us, I'd have to say that Laine is more sophisticated. Maybe because of the lifestyle she leads — getting to ride around in limos and going to openings of Broadway plays. And she always looks fantastic. Like, right now, she was wearing this amazing black pants suit. It was made from stretchy cotton. The bottoms of the legs were cuffed, and the top was short-cropped. She was wearing a leopard-skin leotard under the top. Her fluffy brown hair had been permed several weeks earlier and had grown out to that perfect stage. From her ears dangled tear-drop-shaped blue and green stones, and on one wrist were about twenty silver bangle bracelets.

Even so, Laine somehow seemed very young and innocent just then. Something in her brown eyes reminded me of Grace when she's scared.

Laine cleared her throat. "Um," she began, "nothing like this has ever happened to me. Mom and Dad have never had a huge fight. They argue sometimes, but mostly they get along really well. They spend time together whenever they can, and every now and then I'll catch them exchanging these really private looks that tell me they're still in love with each other. Just like they probably did when they were younger and first got married."

"You know what?" I whispered. "I'm not sure my parents are in love anymore. I mean — "

"Oh, they must be," Laine interrupted.

"They've just hit a bad patch. That's what my aunt would say. You'll see. Everything will be fine soon."

"Yeah. Of course. You're right. I'm sure of it," I replied. "This was probably just a worse fight than usual."

"What started it?" asked Laine. "Do you know?"

"I'm not sure," I replied. "But when I got to our door, Dad was shouting about these huge bills he was getting for the jewelry Mom charges. And believe me, it isn't costume jewelry. It's *really nice* stuff. Like from the antique collection at Altman's, or from Tiffany's. What Dad said is true. Mom *does* shop too much. And she spends too much money on things we don't need. And what Mom said is true, too. She's bored. She does miss having Dad around. He really has become a workaholic. You know, I think everything would seem less awful if Mom and Dad were being ridiculous; if they were tossing silly insults at each other or saying things that *weren't* true."

Laine was toying with one of her earrings. She kept taking it out of her ear, then putting it back in. "I don't know what to say to you," she told me.

I was beginning to cry again. "That's okay."

18

We both sat there for a few moments. I looked at my watch. It was ten of six. Mom and Dad probably weren't worried about me yet. The Walkers hadn't been sure how long they'd be at the gallery, so at breakfast that morning I'd said I'd be home around six. Mom and I knew that meant anywhere from five-thirty till six-thirty.

I sighed. "Laine?" I said in a weary voice.

"Yeah?"

"I'm scared. I'm really scared."

"Maybe," Laine began uncertainly, "you should call Claudia."

"Claudia's parents hardly *ever* fight," I told her.

"But you might feel better if you talked to — to your other best friend."

I managed a tiny smile. "Maybe," I replied. "The Baby-sitters Club is having a meeting right now. I could talk to Dawn and Mary Anne and everybody!" I began to feel better even before Laine handed me her phone.

CHAPTER 3

Before I tell you about my phone call to Claudia, maybe I better tell you a little more about the club and the girls in it. And the best place to start is with Kristy Thomas, I think. That's because Kristy is the president and founder of the club. It was her idea and she made it happen. See, Kristy has three brothers. Two of them are older (they go to high school), and one of them is much younger. A year or so ago, when David Michael, the little one, was just six, I had recently moved to Stoneybrook. Kristy and I were twelve and beginning seventh grade. At that time, the three older Thomas kids were in charge of taking care of David Michael most afternoons. But a day came when none of them was free to watch him, so Mrs. Thomas got on the phone and made call after call, trying to find a sitter. While that was going on, Kristy got one of the brilliant ideas she's famous for. What a waste of time, she thought, that her mom had to make so many calls. It would be much more efficient if a parent could make just one call and reach a bunch of baby-sitters at once. So Kristy got together with her good friends Mary Anne Spier and Claudia Kishi (Kristy lived in their neighborhood then — next door to Mary Anne and across the street from Claud), and they decided to form the Baby-sitters Club. One of the very first things they agreed on was that they needed at least one more member, so Claudia suggested me. Claud and I were just getting to know each other in school, and I'd done my share of baby-sitting here in New York before we moved. The girls accepted me into the club, and after a very casual election, Kristy became the president (that was only fair), Claudia became the vice-president, Mary Anne became the secretary, and I became the treasurer.

The four of us agreed to meet three afternoons a week from five-thirty until six. Parents could call us during those times to line up sitters. How would they know they could reach us then? Because Big-Idea Kristy organized an advertising campaign. By the time we held our first meeting, people had heard about us. We got job calls right away.

I think one reason the club is so successful is because of the businesslike way in which Kristy insists that it run. The club members keep a record book and a notebook. The record book is where important information is noted, and where Mary Anne, the secretary, schedules jobs for the club members. The notebook is more like a diary. In it, each member is responsible for writing up every single job she goes on. And once a week, she's responsible for reading about the experiences the others have had. Hardly anyone likes writing in the book, but we all agreed that knowing what was going on with the families we sat for was really helpful.

Now let me tell you more about the girls in the club, and how the club grew from four members to seven (if you count me as a branch member). I'll start with Kristy again. Boy, are Kristy and I different from each other. If it weren't for the club, I bet we wouldn't have become friends. Kristy is a tomboy. She loves sports, she doesn't care about clothes, and she's athletic and wiry and the shortest kid in her class. She's also, as I've said, full of big ideas — and she usually manages to pull them off. Kristy can be immature and a loudmouth, but she's also funny, a good friend, and an excellent baby-sitter. She's great with kids.

Kristy's home life has not always been easy. Her father ran out on her family when David Michael was pretty little, and her mom had to work hard to keep the rest of the Thomases together. But she managed. And then, around the time the club was starting up, Mrs. Thomas met and fell in love with Watson Brewer, this divorced millionaire. Watson has two adorable children, Andrew and Karen, who live with their mother most of the time and who were three and five then, but Kristy wouldn't have anything to do with them or Watson. She wanted her life to stay the way it was. It didn't, though. The next summer, after school had ended, Kristy's mother and Watson got married and the Thomases moved into the Brewer mansion across town. And recently, the Brewers adopted a little girl, so on the weekends when Karen and Andrew are visiting their father, the house is pretty full. Somehow, Kristy adjusted to everything.

Claudia Kishi, my Connecticut best friend, is the vice-president of the club. She has her own personal phone and private number, so her room has always been an excellent place to hold club meetings. Claudia and I are alike in several major ways, which is probably why we first became friends. For one thing, we are both pretty sophisticated, almost as sophisticated as Laine. (I hope that doesn't sound stuck-up. It's just the truth). For another, we like fashion and clothes and dressing in wild outfits. I think Claud is one of the most beautiful people I've ever seen. She's Japanese-American, and has long silky black hair, dark almond-shaped eyes, and a complexion that's to die for. I don't know how she manages that great complexion, considering all the junk food she eats. She's lucky her complexion is good and that she's so slender. If she got pimply and overweight, it would be a dead giveaway that she's hiding all that stuff in her room that she's not supposed to eat — Ring-Dings, Ding-Dongs, Ho-Hos, potato chips, candy, and more. Her parents don't approve of Claud's junk-food addiction, but as far as I'm concerned, it's just an interesting habit of hers.

The other things you should know about her are that she's a gifted artist, she likes to read Nancy Drew mysteries, and she's a terrible student. The bad-student thing is unfortunate for two reasons. One, Claud has a perfectly good mind; she just doesn't apply herself in school. Two, her older sister Janine is a genius. She's so smart that even though she's still in high school, she's already taking courses at Stoneybrook's community college.

Although Claud loves her parents and her sister, she's had a rough time lately. Recently, her grandmother Mimi died. Claudia and Mimi had been extremely close. For Claudia, losing Mimi was like losing one of her parents. But she's dealing with it pretty well.

The club secretary is Mary Anne Spier. Mary Anne is more like Kristy than Claudia or me, although she's not exactly like any club member. She's like Kristy in that she actually *looks* like her — brown hair, brown eyes, very short. And for the longest time, she cared absolutely zero about clothes. No, wait. That's not true. She dressed like a baby, but that was because her father made her dress that way, not because she didn't care. See, Mr. Spier has raised Mary Anne alone ever since Mrs. Spier died, which was when Mary Anne was very little. And for the longest time, he thought that the best way to raise a daughter alone was to be really strict with her. He made up all these rules for Mary Anne, like she had to wear her hair in braids and she couldn't talk on the phone after dinner unless it was about homework. Lately, though, Mr. Spier has loosened up. He's relaxed his rules, and Mary Anne can wear the clothes she likes and fix her hair however she wants.

Oddly enough, Mary Anne is the only one of the club members with a steady boyfriend. His name is Logan Bruno and he's one of the nicest people I know. He's an associate member of the club. That means he doesn't attend meetings, but he can be called on to take a job if one is offered to the club that none of the other members can take. That happens sometimes. (There's one other associate club member, by the way. She's a friend of Kristy's, named Shannon Kilbourne.)

Mary Anne and her dad live in the house across from Claudia's with their kitten, Tigger. And I have to add that, despite her problems, Mary Anne is the most sincere, compassionate person I know, and a good listener. She's also a big crier and very romantic. She's best friends both with Kristy and with Dawn Schafer.

When did Dawn join the club? Good question. Dawn came along soon after she moved to Stoneybrook, at a time when the club was expanding and needed a fifth member. Dawn moved to Connecticut from California with her mother and her brother Jeff, because Mrs.

Schafer grew up there and her parents still lived there. The move was difficult for Dawn, but even more difficult for Jeff. He never adjusted and finally went back to California to live with his dad. So Dawn's family is split in half.

Like Kristy, Dawn seems to have adjusted, though. She may look fragile, with her long pale blonde hair and her bright blue eyes, but she's tough. And she's a real individual. She dresses the way she pleases (I think of her style as California casual), eats only healthy foods (none of Claud's junk food and no meat), and doesn't care what people think of her. Two interesting things about Dawn: one, she lives in a really old house with a secret passage in it that just might be haunted and two, her mom and Mary Anne's dad have been going out on lots of dates!

Dawn joined the club as an alternate officer, meaning she could take over the job of any club member who couldn't make a meeting, but when I moved back to New York, Dawn became the treasurer.

Something else happened when I moved back to New York. The club's business had been growing and growing, so Kristy decided I would have to be replaced. She ended up replacing me with *two* people — Mallory Pike and Jessi Ramsey. That's because Mal and Jessi are two years younger than the rest of us. They're in sixth grade, and not allowed to sit at night unless it's for their own younger brothers and sisters. But they're good sitters, so Kristy figured that if they could take on a lot of the afternoon jobs, the others would be freed up for evening jobs. So far, the junior officers seem to be working out just fine.

Mallory is somebody the club used to sit *for*. Believe it or not, she has seven younger brothers and sisters — and three of the boys are identical triplets! Mal is wonderful at keeping a level head and staying calm during emergencies. I guess she learned those things just from being the oldest of eight kids.

Mallory is really neat. She loves to read, write, and draw, and is thinking of becoming an author and illustrator of children's books one day. She has one big problem, though. She thinks her parents treat her like a baby. Maybe they do, maybe they don't. *I* think Mal has just reached that difficult age when she feels more grown-up than her parents think she is. Mal really had to work to convince Mr. and Mrs. Pike to allow her to get her ears pierced and her long curly hair cut. And they put their foot down (feet down?) when Mal asked for contacts instead of the glasses she wears. Plus, now she has to get braces. I wish Mal felt better about the way she looks, but as she once said, being eleven is a real trial. Mal copes as best she can.

One thing that helped Mal a lot was making her first best friend. Guess who her best friend is — Jessi Ramsey. Mal and Jessi found each other when they both needed a best friend pretty badly. Mal was going through a hard time trying to grow up, and Jessi and her family had moved to Stoneybrook (right into my old house!) from a little town in New Jersey after the company for which Mr. Ramsey works transferred him to their Stamford, Connecticut, office. Boy, did Jessi have a hard time adjusting to the move. The Ramseys are black, and their neighborhood in New Jersey was pretty integrated. So was the school that Jessi and her younger sister Becca had gone to. But Stoneybrook is almost all white. There are only a few black kids in Stoneybrook Middle School, and none except for Jessi in the sixth grade. I have to say that the people of Stoneybrook did not exactly accept the Ramseys right away. They didn't look closely enough to see what a nice family they are. They only saw their dark skin. (Well, that was at first. Things are better now.) But in the beginning, it would have helped if they'd kept their minds open. If they had, they would have found two parents who care about their kids very much. They would have found Becca, who is eight and extremely shy, but a loyal friend and a good student. They would have found Squirt, the baby of the family, who is adorable. His real name is John Philip Ramsey, Jr., but when he was born, he was so tiny that the nurses in the hospital nicknamed him Squirt. (He's caught up to other babies his age now.) And they would have found Jessi. Jessi loves kids, horses, and dancing. She's a great baby-sitter, she and Mal read horse stories nonstop (especially the ones by Marguerite Henry), and boy, can Jessi dance. Jessi has taken ballet forever. When her family moved to Connecticut, she was accepted by this really good dancing school in Stamford where she goes for lessons twice a week. She has these long, long legs and she practices, practices, practices. She has even danced onstage in front of big audiences.

So those were the people I knew I'd be reaching when I picked up the phone in Laine's room — Claudia, Kristy, Mary Anne, Dawn, Mal, and Jessi. Some of them were closer friends than others, but they were all my friends.

The phone rang twice.

A familiar voice answered it.

"Hello, Claud?" I said.

CHAPTER 4

Wednesday

Today I was so exited! Stacy called!
I no this isnt' a babysiting ex ex expuryence,
Kristy, but its club bisness so Im writting
about it anyway. Anyway waht I mean to say
is I was exited when Stacey frist called
but then it sounded lick the new york
barnch of the BSC is having some probelms
at home we all tryed to help her. I am sure
things will work out. At least I hop so.

I was a little nervous about calling right in the middle of a BSC meeting. Kristy likes the meetings to be strictly meetings — since they *are* only half an hour long — and she doesn't like to tie up the phone with nonclub business. But nobody seemed to mind my call *too* much (especially not Claudia).

"Stacey?" Claudia replied, after I'd said hello.

"Yeah, it's me."

Right away, Claudia's emotional antennae must have gone up. Mary Anne's are always up (that's why she's so sensitive to people), but Claud's come up instantly when someone she cares about is having a hard time. "What's wrong?" she asked. "Something's wrong, isn't it?"

"Yes. Can you talk for a minute? I know I called during a meeting, but . . ."

"Just a sec," said Claudia hurriedly.

I heard some funny sounds. First a muffled one that was probably Claud putting her hand over the receiver, then some scufflings and murmurings that were probably Claudia and Kristy arguing over whether to allow a personal call during a meeting. Claudia won quickly.

"Hi, Stace," she said, a bit breathlessly. "Okay, go ahead. What's wrong?"

"Well," I began, "it's — it's my parents." This was hard to talk about over the phone. I wished my friends were right there with me.

"Your parents?" Claudia repeated. "Is one of them sick or something?"

"Oh, no. Nothing like that." (I knew Claud was thinking of Mimi, the hospital, and the funeral.) "It's just that they fight so much. And the fights are getting bigger. Today I came home and Dad was already there and I stood out in the hallway and listened to them yell at each other. They were yelling awful things, Claud."

"What kinds of things?" she whispered.

I told her about the jewelry bills and Mom calling Dad a workaholic and everything else I could remember.

"Gosh," said Claudia when I'd finished. "That sounds serious."

"I know," I replied. I could feel the tears starting again, but I don't like to cry over the phone, so I put a stop to them.

"I'm not sure what to say," Claud went on. "My parents have never had a fight like that. They always just try to discuss things. You know what? Maybe you should talk to Dawn.

Her parents fought a lot before she left California. Nobody else's parents have big problems." Claudia paused. "What?" she said to somebody in the background. Then, "Oh." She got back on the phone. "Kristy says to tell you that when her real father was living with them the Thomases fought an awful lot, but Kristy was too little to remember much of it. Here, let me put Dawn on."

There were more scufflings and murmurings in the background, and I pictured Kristy looking at Claud's clock and tapping her fingers on the arm of the director's chair I was sure she was sitting in. (She always sits in the director's chair, wearing a visor.) But after just a moment, Dawn was on the phone.

"Hi, Stace," she said. "I'm really sorry you're having some problems."

"Thanks," I replied, "but it's my parents, not me."

"When they make you feel bad, it's your problem, too. Believe me, I know. So what's going on?"

"What isn't?" I answered bitterly. I wanted to tell Dawn everything, but suddenly I just couldn't. That mental picture of an impatient Kristy kept creeping into my mind. Plus, I felt funny telling Dawn my parents' business. In fact, I felt pretty funny knowing that the entire club already knew my business. I wanted their comfort and support — but I didn't necessarily want to turn myself inside out for it. Maybe calling during a meeting hadn't been such a good idea after all.

I cleared my throat. "Well, Mom and Dad are just fighting all the time," I told Dawn. "Over everything."

"Money and stuff?"

"Yeah," I said.

"Their relationship?"

"Yeah."

"You?"

"Yeah."

"Oh, that's a bad sign."

Okay, enough of this. I changed the subject immediately. "So how's Jeff?"

"Jeff? My brother?"

"Who else?"

We giggled. Maybe the conversation had been getting too heavy for both of us.

"He's fine," said Dawn. "Mom and Dad let us call each other whenever we want, but it's hard because of the time difference. I can't call too early in the morning because then it's *really* early in California, and Jeff can't call after eight at night because it's after eleven here. Still, he's back in California with Dad, which is great for him. . . . What?" (Another conversation with someone at the meeting.) Then, "Stace? Mary Anne wants to say hello, okay?"

"Sure." I turned to Laine while I waited for Mary Anne, and said, "I'll pay you back every penny of this call. I promise."

Laine smiled. "No problem," she said.

"Stacey?" I heard an excited voice in my ear. It was Mary Anne's, and it occurred to me that the last time I'd spoken to any of my Stoneybrook friends, except for Claudia, had been on the day of Mimi's funeral. I wished we could talk or get together under *ordinary* circumstances.

"Hi, Mary Anne!" I tried to liven up a bit.

"You want to talk?" she asked gently.

"Yes," I replied, "but not about Mom and Dad anymore."

"Okay." (This is one thing I love about Mary Anne. She doesn't press issues, and she respects people's wishes.)

"So how's Logan?" I asked.

"Oh, he's fine. Or, as Logan would say, he's 'fan.' " We laughed. Logan is from Louisville, Kentucky, and has this neat southern accent.

"And Tigger?"

"He's fine, too. He caught a mouse yesterday."

"In your *house*?" I asked, aghast. Sometimes roaches get into our apartment, but I've never seen anything with a tail.

"*No!* Outdoors. The mouse was outdoors. Although Tigger brought it inside and dropped it in his food dish."

"You're kidding!"

"Nope. It was so disgusting. Oh, wait. Kristy wants to say hello."

I looked at my watch. It was six o'clock. I'd wasted the rest of their meeting. Oh, well. Kristy couldn't be too mad if she still wanted to say hi to me.

"Stace?" said Kristy's voice.

"Hi. Sorry about tying up the club phone."

"Oh, that's all right. How are you doing?"

"Okay, I guess. How are the Krushers?" Kristy coaches a softball team for little kids in Stoneybrook. The team is called Kristy's Krushers.

"Not bad, considering. We get closer and closer to beating Bart's Bashers."

"How's our walking disaster?"

"Jackie Rodowsky? Just the same. I baby-sat for him last week and he rode his bike right into the garage wall, skinned his knees, broke a flowerpot, and later dropped a pizza on the floor. At least he didn't drop it on a rug."

"Poor kid," I said, but I couldn't help laughing a little.

"I know," answered Kristy. "Listen, Jessi and Mal both want to say hi and then we'll have to go. Well, except for Claudia. It's after six."

"Okay," I replied. So I talked to Jessi and asked about her dancing, and about Becca and Squirt. "Hey, how's Charlotte?" I wanted to know. Charlotte Johanssen is Becca Ramsey's best friend, and my favorite Stoneybrook kid to sit for. She's eight years old, and she's shy and creative, just like Grace and Henry. Sometimes I really miss her.

"Charlotte just got over tonsillitis, but — "

"Tonsillitis! Is she going to have her tonsils out?"

"Nope. Not yet anyway. Don't worry. She's fine now. She and Becca dressed up like grown-ups yesterday and spent the afternoon playing office. It looked horribly boring, but they kept it up for hours. . . . Oh, here's Mal. 'Bye, Stacey."

" 'Bye, Jessi. . . . Hi, Mal."

"Hi, Stacey. Guess what. Claire was asking about you the other day."

"Claire was?" (Claire is the youngest kid in Mal's family. I got to know all the Pikes pretty well when I went on two vacations with them as a mother's helper.) "What did she say?"

"She said, 'I miss Stacey-silly-billy-goo-goo.'"

Mal and I both laughed. And at that moment, I missed Claire and my Stoneybrook friends a lot. But I knew it was time to get off the phone. The BSC meeting was over, and if I didn't get home by six-thirty my parents would probably call the police.

I had to hang up the phone. I couldn't put it off any longer. The only good thing about leaving Laine's apartment was that no one yelled, "Have fun and be careful!" as I walked out the door, which is what my mother used to do every single time she let me out of her sight in New York.

There was just Laine saying, "I know things will be okay."

And on the way home I managed to convince myself that Laine was right and that I was being melodramatic.

CHAPTER 5

As right as I hoped Laine was, I still approached my apartment apprehensively. At least I managed to be civil to James and the guys at the desk.

"Hi, James," I said. "Hi, Isaac. Hi, Lloyd."

The three of them looked relieved to find me acting normal again.

I rang for the elevator. It crashed to the ground floor, the doors jarred themselves open, I pressed the button for the 12th floor, the doors closed with a bang, and up I flew. When I was little, I used to jump around on the elevator while it was moving, which made my body feel heavier or lighter (depending on whether I was going up or down). Then Laine told me that jumping could make the cable break and the elevator crash, so I stopped, even though I think she made that up.

The doors opened on my floor. I stepped

into the hallway and paused, listening. The only sound was the TV blaring in 12C.

I walked to my apartment on tiptoe, stopping every few feet.

Still I heard nothing but the sounds of *I Love Lucy*.

At 12E I listened especially carefully. Nothing.

I found my key, slipped it in the lock, and let myself inside. A tiny part of me was afraid that something had happened, that Mom or Dad had stormed off. But, no. They were sitting in the living room. They didn't look like they were doing much of anything, so they must have been talking.

Whew. If they were talking, that meant they weren't fighting.

"Hi, Mom. Hi, Dad," I said casually, as if I'd just left the Walkers' apartment, hadn't heard the fight, and hadn't been to Laine's.

"Hi, honey," they replied at the same time.

Another good sign. Speaking in unison.

But then Mom said, "Stacey, we need to talk to you."

Whoa, bad sign.

"You do?" I desperately hoped that they were going to accuse me of not sticking to my diet. I even hoped that my English teacher had called up personally to tell my parents about the D I'd gotten on a quiz.

No such luck. I sat down on the edge of a couch and looked at Mom and Dad, who were glancing at each other as if to say, "You go first." "No, *you* go first."

Finally, Mom went first. "I guess it's no secret," she said, "that your dad and I have been having some problems."

No secret? The whole building probably knew.

"Well, I have heard you, um, arguing a lot lately," I admitted.

Mom nodded. "And we've decided to do something about it. Stacey, your father and I are getting a divorce."

"What?" I whispered.

"We're getting a divorce," Dad spoke up.

I felt as if someone had slapped me across the face. I actually put my hand up to my cheek. Mom must have thought I was going to cry, because she rushed to my side and started to put her arms around me. I pushed her away, though. I was angry, not upset.

"Why?" I demanded. "You don't need a divorce." But I think I knew that they *did*.

Otherwise, I wouldn't have shouted, "Can't you work things out like two adults? That's what you always say to me when I'm having a fight with a friend." I was protesting too much. Isn't that how the saying goes?

"Honey, we *are* working things out," Mom told me. "The divorce is our solution."

"We've been having trouble for a long time now," Dad added. "Ever since I got the news that I was being transferred to Stoneybrook."

For that long? Why hadn't I noticed earlier? Because I'd been too busy baby-sitting and making friends and taking vacations and going to camp and shopping and doing homework, I guessed.

"My job has been on shaky territory since the first transfer," said Dad.

That much I knew.

"I guess the shakiness spread to our marriage," he went on. "I feel as if I've got to work harder than ever just to keep from being fired. Your mother thinks I should look for a new job."

I thought she thought Dad was a workaholic.

"There are other problems," added Mom. "Money, that sort of thing."

They were being vague to protect me, I decided. If only they knew what I already knew, but this wasn't the time to admit I'd been eavesdropping.

"Those problems sound big, but not — not unworkable," I said hopefully. "Can't you reach some compromises? I know! You could see a marriage counselor!"

"We have seen one," said Mom.

"And?"

"And she was very helpful. We've been seeing her for three months. She was the one who suggested we get the divorce."

"Oh. So you saw a divorce counselor," I snapped.

"Stacey, don't be difficult," said Dad. "This doctor is well respected and we liked her very much."

"I haven't even met her and already I hate her," I told my father.

He ignored my comment. "She knows about our problems, our lives, you, even our finances. After she suggested that a divorce was probably the best solution to our problems, she helped us arrange as amicable a divorce as possible."

"What's that supposed to mean?" I asked.

"It means splitting up with as little trouble as we can, and making things as easy on you as we can."

"Could we please backtrack for a second?" I said.

But Mom changed the subject. "Stacey, have you given yourself your insulin today?"

"Of course I have."

"Just checking." Mom looked at her watch. "It's dinnertime," she added.

"I'm not hungry," I said.

"You have to eat anyway." Mom was losing her patience.

She was right, though. I did have to eat. With my kind of diabetes, I can't skip meals. I have to eat regularly, eat what the doctor says, and take in a certain number of calories every day. It's such a drag. If I don't do those things, my blood sugar gets out of whack and I'm in trouble.

"Come on," said Mom. "We can continue this discussion over dinner. I ordered in from the deli."

"Unnecessary expense," muttered Dad, but neither Mom nor I said anything.

Mom had ordered several different kinds of salad and some plain sandwiches — lean meats on whole wheat bread. Healthy stuff that I could eat. She'd set a bowl of fruit out, too, and I knew I was supposed to eat an apple or a banana with dinner. So I filled up my plate, even though I had no appetite at all.

The three of us sat around the kitchen table with the remains of the deli food in a jumble on a nearby counter. Actually, I don't think *any* of us was hungry, but we all began to eat.

"Now, what was it you wanted to ask?" said Mom.

"I wanted to know more about your problems," I replied. "I mean, if you can tell me. I want to know just what it is that's so big you can't work it out."

"Stacey, it's a lot of things," said my father.

"And," added Mom, "some of them you probably wouldn't — "

"Wouldn't understand?" I interrupted. "Listen, I'm not a baby anymore. I'm thirteen years old."

"It's not that," said my mother. "I don't think anyone except your father and I could understand some of these things. They're personal. They have to do with our feelings toward each other. And those feelings have changed."

"Are you in love anymore?" I asked suddenly. "Are you?"

Mom and Dad glanced at each other.

There was a pause.

At last Dad said, "Your mother and I will always care about each other. We'll always love each other — and we'll love you, of course. But no, we're not *in* love anymore."

I felt stung. I looked down at my plate. It was mostly full, so I began shoveling in the food. The faster I ate, the faster I could leave the table. While I was eating (and listening to myself chew, since no one was talking), I realized that my parents hadn't really answered my original question.

"Please tell me more about your problems," I said firmly. I didn't look at my parents, just at my plate, which was growing cleaner by the moment.

I heard Dad say, "Mostly we just have differences, Stace."

"Irreconcilable ones," added Mom. "We are not meant to be living together any longer."

That did it. I was pretty much finished with my dinner by then, so I banged my fork onto the table, stood up, threw down my napkin, and stalked away without excusing myself.

I stalked right into my bedroom and slammed the door shut. I slammed it so hard

I could feel my walls shake. The china figures on my dresser rattled.

I locked my door.

Then I switched on my stereo. I put my loudest tape in the tape deck, turned the volume up as high as it would go, and blasted out my eardrums for a minute or two. But I turned the volume down before any of the neighbors could complain.

Mom and Dad knocked on my door five times that night. I wouldn't answer them. I wouldn't leave my room, either. At ten-thirty, I fell asleep with my clothes on. I didn't wake up until seven o'clock the next morning.

CHAPTER 6

Thursday was the most awful morning of my life. My body felt grungy because I'd spent the night in my clothes, and my mouth felt like an old sock. It tasted the way I imagined an old sock would taste, too.

Groggily, I rolled out of bed, tripping over my sneakers, which were lying on their sides next to the bed. I turned off the power on my stereo and looked out my window. (I hadn't bothered to close the blinds the night before.)

Outside I saw a chilly gray day.

Perfect, I thought. The day fit my mood.

I made my way to the door of my bedroom and listened for a moment. I wanted to put off running into Mom or Dad for as long as possible. I didn't hear a sound. Had Dad already left for work? He usually left early — but not by seven o'clock.

I dared to open my door. Then I tiptoed into

the hallway and peeked into the living room.

My father was asleep on the couch! He and Mom didn't even share their bedroom anymore. How awful. How long had that been going on? I wondered. And did Mom ever sleep on the couch or was it all up to Dad? I turned away, sure I had seen something I wasn't supposed to have seen. But it couldn't be helped. We'd all overslept a little that morning.

I retreated to the bathroom, where I locked myself in. (I seemed to feel more secure locked into places.) I took a long, hot shower and washed my hair twice. Afterward, I brushed my teeth two or three times, trying to get rid of the old-sock taste. While I was brushing, a knock sounded at the door.

"Morning, honey!" called Mom's voice. "Why don't you take it easy today? You don't have to go to school if you don't want to."

In answer, I turned the water on as hard as it would go.

A few moments later I was locked in my room again, trying to decide what to wear. I was going to school, of course. There was no way I would stay at home with either Mom or Dad. (I was pretty sure they wouldn't *both* be there.)

Another knock.

This time Dad's voice called, "Hi, Stace! How do bacon and eggs sound for breakfast? I'll cook. I'm going to the office a little later than usual this morning."

I kept my mouth shut.

I had never, ever felt so angry at my parents. Not even when they had dragged me to this awful doctor who wanted to change my whole life around in order to help my diabetes.

Dad waited for my answer. When he didn't get one, he left. I heard his footsteps retreat into the living room on his way to the kitchen.

I dressed. I put on one of my better outfits — short red pants with purple suspenders over a bright yellow and black sweat shirt. On my feet I put my purple push-down socks and a pair of red hightop sneakers.

I added jewelry — a big necklace with wooden bananas and oranges strung on it, and dangly earrings shaped like sunglasses.

I fixed my hair. I brushed it until it was full and shiny. Then I rolled up a red scarf and tied it in my hair like a headband. My outfit was pretty colorful. I think I was trying to make up for the gray day.

After I had tied the scarf in my hair, I was ready for school. I wished I could just beam myself there like they do on *Star Trek*. That way, I wouldn't have to see my parents. But obviously, I couldn't beam myself anywhere. Even if I could have, what would have been the point? I'd have to face Mom and Dad sooner or later.

So I did. I unlocked my door and walked into the kitchen.

"Good morning!" said my parents.

Mom was setting the table. Dad was standing over the stove, turning bacon and stirring a pan of scrambled eggs.

I took my glass from the table, filled it with orange juice, got a bagel out of the refrigerator and a banana from the fruit bowl, and sat down to my own version of breakfast.

"No eggs?" said Dad at the same moment that Mom said, "No bacon?"

I pulled an old trick. I reached over to the counter and picked up *The New York Times*. I opened it and pretended to read, but mostly I just concentrated on eating fast.

Mom and Dad tried several more times to talk to me.

"We know you're mad," said Mom. (No kidding.)

"We understand," said Dad. (Do you? Do you *really?*)

After that, they lapsed into silence.

As soon as possible, I left the table, gave my teeth another brushing, gathered up my schoolbooks, put on my blue-jean jacket, and walked out the door. For once in her life, my mother didn't call after me to have fun and be careful.

Even though I didn't have any time to spare, I dawdled on the way to school. I wanted to think about things. I hadn't done my homework the night before, so what did it matter if I got to school late, anyway? Besides, knowing Mom and Dad, one of them was calling my guidance counselor right now to tell her what was going on. I would probably get some special treatment for awhile, I thought, as I left our block and made a right onto a busy avenue.

Caitlin did. Keith did. Shayla did.

Who are Caitlin, Keith, and Shayla? They're kids in my grade whose parents got divorced earlier in the year. Think of it. Three other divorces right in the eighth grade. I sure wasn't the only divorced kid around. (That's what Caitlin and Shayla call themselves — divorced kids, meaning kids with divorced parents.) But that didn't make me any less angry. In fact, it made me more angry.

What was wrong with parents these days? Why couldn't they get married and stay married like parents did in olden times? Whatever happened to commitment? What happened to "forever"? To "till death do us part"? Really, someone ought to rewrite the wedding vows so that the bride and groom say, "Till divorce do us part."

Even while I was thinking those things, though, I was remembering something I'd heard Caitlin say at the beginning of the year. She'd said, "I'm *glad* my parents are getting divorced. Now I won't have to listen to their fights."

I'd thought she'd just been saying that, that she hadn't meant it. But now I wasn't so sure. I wouldn't mind an end to the arguing.

But I still didn't want Mom and Dad to get divorced.

I entered my homeroom five minutes after the first bell had rung.

Mrs. Kaufman, my homeroom teacher, looked up at me, smiled, then continued reading the morning announcements.

So one of my parents *had* called the school. Mrs. Kaufman knew. If she hadn't known, she would have stopped reading the announcements and asked why I was late. She always does that. And if a kid doesn't have a written excuse, she cooks up some sort of punishment. She never just smiles and continues with what she's doing.

I spent that day in a fog. I barely spoke to anyone. And I was constantly dreaming up ways not to have to see my friends. I just couldn't face telling them the news yet. I took different routes to my classes and to my locker. When I had to use the bathroom, I went to this old one on the first floor that's used mostly by teachers. I even hit on a way to avoid Laine in the cafeteria at lunchtime. See, we have sixth period lunch. So at the beginning of fifth period, I asked my science teacher if I could go to the library to work on a project. Then, instead of going to the library, I went to the cafeteria and ate a very fast lunch. As soon as I was done I really did go to the library. I stayed there right through sixth period, holed up at a desk in a remote corner behind shelves of books about sociology.

I did a lot of thinking and absolutely no work. This is what I was thinking:

When Caitlin's parents got divorced, her father moved out and her mother stayed in their apartment.

When Keith's parents got divorced, *his* father moved out ánd *his* mother stayed in *their* apartment.

And when Shayla's parents got divorced, *her* father moved out and *her* mother stayed in *their* apartment.

Where, I wondered, would Dad go?

Then I thought of something else. I'd heard Mom say the day before that she wanted to leave the city. Had she meant that she wanted our whole family to move, maybe as a way of trying to save the marriage? Or did she still want to move, without Dad? If she moved, would I have to go with her? Did kids ever get to stay with their fathers? Would Dad keep our apartment or find another one?

Other thoughts crowded into my head. I thought of the Trip-Man. The Trip-Man is this awful guy that Dawn Schafer's mother dated a lot. And he wasn't the only man she'd dated since she moved back to Stoneybrook. There was Mary Anne's father, and there were some other men.

What if I were living with my mom and she married someone I hated? I'd have a wicked stepfather. What if he had kids I hated? I'd have wicked stepsisters and stepbrothers.

Suddenly, I felt lost. No one had died or left

me, but I felt as if I were on a lake in a boat and had fallen overboard with no life vest, and didn't know how to swim.

I knew divorce was pretty common. Look at Caitlin, Keith, and Shayla. Look at all the other kids in my grade whose parents had already gotten divorced. Look at Dawn. Look at Kristy. The divorce rate is fifty percent. I read that somewhere. That means that about half of all couples who get married will eventually get divorced.

And still, I felt embarrassed.

I knew that was why I'd avoided Laine. I was embarrassed — and angry. I couldn't face telling her the awful news yet. Besides, I had too many unanswered questions such as, Where will I live? Whom will I live with? What happens if I wind up with a stepparent I don't like?

I was truly miserable. All I wanted was to turn the clock back twenty-four hours to the day before and let things go on as they'd been going on, fights and all. I decided I would rather have fights than a divorce.

I did not want any changes.

CHAPTER 7

Somehow, I managed to avoid Laine all day. It wasn't easy, considering we have the last class of the afternoon together. But I made sure I got to class late (of course, my teacher didn't care), and then when the bell rang, I gathered up my things and raced to Mr. Berlenbach's desk. I pretended I didn't understand what we'd covered in class that day. We got into a long discussion. When it looked like Laine might wait for me, since she was hovering around the door, I waved her on.

Five minutes later, I left Mr. Berlenbach's room and walked toward our apartment building in peace. Well, in as much peace as you can find on busy New York streets. I took my time. I didn't have a baby-sitting job that afternoon, but that didn't mean I had to go right home.

Suddenly an idea came to me. I found some change in my purse, headed for a pay phone, and called home.

Mom answered.

In a rush, I informed her that I was going to spend the afternoon at the library, but that I'd be home for dinner. I didn't give her a chance to say much. She got as far as, "All right, but Stacey — "

And I said, "See you later. 'Bye," and hung up.

Of course I didn't go to the library. Instead I just dawdled around. I walked over to Columbus Avenue and browsed through some of the kitschy stores there. I looked in The Last Wound-Up and in this store that sells big everything — pencils the size of baseball bats, paper clips that an elephant could use, golf balls that look more like beach balls, that sort of thing. I wandered through clothing stores and card stores. I bought a diet soda from a street vendor.

When at last it was near dinnertime, I headed for home. I reached my block and right away I saw Judy. Judy is the street person who lives in our neighborhood — outdoors. She's homeless. She literally *lives* on the *street*. When it gets super cold, she goes to a shelter for awhile, but she always comes back. The people around here sometimes give her money. The restaurant owners and grocery-store owners give her food.

Judy and I have been friends (sort of) ever since Mom and Dad and I moved to this apartment after we left Stoneybrook.

"Hi, Judy," I said listlessly as I approached her.

Judy was sitting right on the cement, surrounded by tattered shopping bags full of . . . I don't know what. It always looked like trash to me. But I knew the things were Judy's personal treasures.

Judy was wearing about seventeen layers of clothes, and was rubbing lotion onto her poor chapped hands and face. I wondered where she'd gotten it.

"Hi, Missy," replied Judy cheerfully. (Missy is what she calls me when she's in a good mood. When she's in a bad mood, she won't answer. Or else she screams out senseless things for hours.)

I looked in my book bag to see if I had anything Judy might want. I handed her a pencil and after several moments, Judy selected a particular shopping bag and poked it inside.

"Thanks," she said when she was finished. "How are you today, Missy?"

"My parents are getting a divorce," I told her.

"Crying shame."

I couldn't tell just what Judy meant by that. Was she being sarcastic?

"That's what's wrong with the world today," Judy went on, sounding wise. "Too much divorce. Too much thieving and pillaging, too. End of civilization."

Whoa. Time to go.

" 'Bye, Judy," I said. "See you tomorrow."

I walked into my building, sailed up to the 12th floor, and crept down our hallway as if I were approaching a firing squad.

It was almost six o'clock. I entered our apartment and, just like the night before, found both of my parents sitting in the living room.

"Hi, Stacey," said Dad at the same time that Mom said, "Hello, honey."

I ignored them and headed for my bedroom. But to my surprise, the door was closed. A sign had been taped to it. It read: DO NOT ENTER. GO BACK TO THE LIVING ROOM AND TALK TO YOUR PARENTS.

With a huge sigh, I dropped my book bag and purse on the floor in the hallway and returned to the living room. I did have to talk to my parents. I knew that. I couldn't ignore them forever.

I plopped into an armchair and looked from Mom to Dad. "What?" I said.

"We have some unfinished business," my father informed me.

"What?" I said again, as if I didn't care at all.

"Aren't you curious about anything?" asked Mom. "Aren't you wondering what's going to happen now? Where we're going to live? Whom you're going to live with? I would be, if I were you."

I shrugged, even though I was *dying* of curiosity.

"Stacey, you must talk to us," said Dad. "We're very sorry about what's happening, but you've had twenty-four hours to absorb the shock. Now we have to go on with things. There are a lot of arrangements to be made, and we'd like your thoughts about some of them."

"Okay, okay." I settled down, putting my feet up on our coffee table, which I am not allowed to do. I just wanted to see what would happen; to see if I'd get any more special treatment.

But Dad said immediately, "Feet on the floor, Anastasia."

Whoa. Anastasia.

I put my feet down in an instant.

"All right," said Mom. "I'll begin." She sent my father a message with her eyes that plainly said, "Okay?"

Dad nodded.

"Well," said Mom. "First of all, the marriage counselor — "

"Divorce counselor," I corrected her.

"Anastasia Elizabeth McGill," said Dad warningly.

I shut my mouth.

"The *marriage* counselor," Mom repeated pointedly, "advised us both to leave the apartment. Your father and I will each be moving."

"You *will?* Why?" I exclaimed.

"Because the counselor said that if one stays here and the other leaves, you might feel that the parent who left had deserted you. So we're both moving."

"Where to?" I asked. And then I blurted out (because I just had to know), "Which one of you will I live with?"

"We're leaving that up to you," Dad replied. "That will be your decision entirely. You won't

64

have any say over where we move to, but you may decide whom to live with."

"Or how to divide your time between us," added Mom.

"Divide my — ?" I started to say. And then I remembered Shayla. I remembered something about "joint custody." Shayla's parents live about ten blocks from each other, and Shayla and her sisters live with their mother from Wednesday afternoons (after school) until Saturday night. Then on Saturday night they go to their father's and stay there until they leave for school on Wednesday. The girls have everything they need at both places, so they hardly have to pack up anything on Wednesdays and Saturdays except schoolbooks. Keith has a different arrangement. His parents also live pretty near each other, but he and his brother spend a month with one, a month with the other, all year long. Caitlin has a third kind of arrangement. Her father moved to a suburb of Chicago after the divorce. Caitlin and her brother live with their mom during the school year, but spend vacations and summers with their dad.

"Are you going to have joint custody of me?" I asked my parents.

"Yes," they replied, looking surprised.

And Dad asked, "How do you know about joint custody?"

"I just do." I paused. "So I can live with either one of you or go back and forth between you — however I want?"

My parents nodded.

"Well, I guess my decision will depend on where you're going to move to," I said, thinking of Caitlin.

"I'll be staying in the city," said Dad, "because of my job."

I looked at Mom, knowing now that she wanted to move. But where to? Long Island? New Jersey? Or maybe as close by as one of the nice neighborhoods in the Bronx. Now that wouldn't be bad at all. She'd still be in the city — technically — but she'd feel almost as if she were in the country.

"I'd kind of like to go back to Stoneybrook," said Mom.

I opened my eyes so wide my eyebrows nearly rose right off the top of my head. "Back to *Stoneybrook?*" I squeaked.

Mom nodded. "I really loved that area. I was very sorry when we left."

"But — but what would you do there?" I asked.

"Find a job. It's high time I went back to work. But not here in the city. Somewhere with a slower pace."

I couldn't believe it. I was all confused. I'd thought that Dad would move out and I'd live in our apartment with Mom half the time and with Dad the rest of the time. That seemed like the best arrangement. Now I had to choose between New York City and Stoneybrook. I also had to choose between my parents. Obviously, I couldn't do what Shayla and Keith do. My arrangement would have to be more like Caitlin's.

"I — I can't make a decision until I know where you're going to live," I said to my parents.

"Fair enough," replied Dad.

"One thing we can assure you," Mom said, "is that we'll both buy or rent places that will be big enough for you. You'll have your own bedroom wherever you go."

"Okay," I said. Thoughts were whirling around in my head. Go back to Stoneybrook? To the Baby-sitters Club and all my friends there? Leave New York again? I had no idea what to do.

"May I go to my room?" I asked. "I need to think."

"After dinner," said Dad. "You need to eat, too."

I gave in quickly. The faster I ate, the faster I could escape.

As soon as dinner was over, I retreated to my room — and the telephone. I didn't have my own phone number, like Claudia does, but at least I had an extension in my room, so I could make private calls.

I phoned Laine first. I told her the news flat-out, pretty much like this: "Hi, Laine. It's me, Stace. My parents are getting a divorce." That was the second time I'd said those awful words out loud, and they were becoming easier to say.

I think Laine nearly dropped the phone. "They're *what?*" she cried. "Oh, Stacey, I'm so sorry." (No wonder she was surprised. We'd been friends for an awfully long time.)

I told her about Mom and Dad's moving plans, and right away I could hear her growing fearful. "Oh, please don't go away again, Stace," she said. "Stay here with your father, okay? It'll be easier anyway."

I didn't know what to say, except that I wouldn't be making a decision for awhile.

Then I called Claudia. Her reaction was a little different. "You're coming back? You're coming back?" she shrieked. "Oh, Stace. Oh, I mean — I mean, I'm sorry. About the divorce. Really. But you're coming *back?* I can't believe it! Oh, please, please, *please* come back!"

"Pretty please? With a cherry on top?" I teased her.

Claudia laughed.

"Listen," I said. "I don't know what I'm doing yet. You know how much I love New York. Besides, Mom isn't positive she wants to go back to Stoneybrook. She's just thinking about it."

At long last I called Dawn for advice. She would be more understanding, I decided. And she wouldn't get all hung up about where I lived. She'd want me to come back to Stoneybrook, but not as badly as Claud did. And she's be a little more sympathetic about the rest of my problems.

"The thing about divorce," she told me, "is waiting. You have to wait for a awful lot — for decisions, lawyers, even movers." (I giggled.) "The best way to look at the situation is to realize that the worst part is over. You know your parents are splitting up. Now it's just a matter of dealing with each new step that comes along."

That was sound advice from practical Dawn. I decided to take the advice and wait — for each of my parents to find a new place to live. Then I would decide what to do next.

CHAPTER 8

"Good-bye, Mommy! Good-bye, Daddy!" called Henry cheerfully.

" 'Bye, Henry," said the Walkers as they headed for their front door. " 'Bye, Grace," they added.

" 'Bye," said Grace in a small voice. She was sniffling.

As much as Grace likes me, she never likes for her parents to leave. She usually cries.

Friday night was no exception.

I picked Grace up and whispered, "Blow a kiss to your mom and dad. Then they'll blow kisses to you in bed when they come home."

"While I'm asleep?" asked Grace, her voice wobbling.

I nodded.

Grace blew noisy kisses after her parents as they closed the door behind them.

"Well," I said, setting Grace down as she

dried her tears, "I better start getting supper ready." I was going to be baby-sitting at the Walkers for a long time that evening. Mr. Walker's show was opening, and it was a big event.

"Is it hot-dog night?" asked Henry excitedly. (He knows that his mother leaves only hot dogs or hamburgers for me to prepare if I have to give the kids dinner when I baby-sit.)

"It certainly is," I replied.

"Oh, boy!" Henry began to jump up and down. (Grace imitated him.) "What a great night!" Henry went on. "Hot dogs for supper, a special cartoon show on TV, and Mommy bought us new pastels today."

That *does* make for an exciting evening, when you're five.

"Okay," I said, "who's hungry?"

"I am! I am!" said Henry.

"I am! I am!" said Grace.

"Good. Let's see. While I fix the hot dogs, you guys can have a table-setting race. I'll time you and tell you how long it takes to set the table." (Just so you know, you can only have a table-setting race when you're using paper plates and cups, and plastic forks and spoons, which is what the Walkers always leave out when a baby-sitter is going to feed the kids.

That way, you don't have to worry about breaking anything.)

Grace grabbed some napkins.

Henry grabbed three paper plates.

"Take your marks, get set . . . GO!" I shouted.

Henry and Grace scurried back and forth between the counter and the table, working frantically, while I turned the hot dogs in the skillet and got milk and applesauce from the refrigerator.

"We're done! We're done!" Grace shrieked suddenly.

I checked my watch. "What do you know?" I said. "You guys just broke your table-setting record! You beat it by three seconds."

"We *did?!* Oh, boy!" cried Henry.

"Good timing," I added, "because supper is just about ready."

I served up the hot dogs and applesauce (not my idea of a great meal, but it *was* easy to fix) and we sat down to eat.

"Do we have any toothpicks?" asked Henry, as he was about to bite into his hot dog.

"I think so," I replied. "Why?"

"You'll see. I can make something." Henry set his hot dog back on his plate and took it out of its bun.

I got up, found a box of toothpicks, and handed it to Henry. Very carefully, he broke several of the toothpicks in half. Then he chopped one end off of his hot dog, stuck four half-toothpicks in the long part, attached the little piece with another half-toothpick, and announced, "Look! I made my hot dog into a dachshund!"

"Hey, that's great!" I exclaimed.

Well, of course, Grace had to turn her hot dog into a dachshund, too, before she could eat it, so supper took a little longer than usual that night. By the time we'd finished, the cartoon show was about to begin.

Henry and Grace settled themselves at a table in front of the TV with a stack of drawing paper and their new pastels. One thing I love about the Walker kids — they almost never just park themselves in front of the TV and stare at it. When they turn it on, they work on a project at the same time.

So the kids colored while I cleaned up the kitchen. When their show was over, Grace said, "Could you please read to us, Stacey?"

"Sure," I replied. "What do you want to hear?"

Henry and Grace have a huge collection of books. That's because Mr. and Mrs. Walker like to read, and also because Mrs. Walker knows a lot about children's books since she illustrates them.

"We want to hear . . . *The Snowy Day*," said Grace.

"And *The Owl and the Pussycat*," added Henry.

"Great," I replied. "Pajamas first. And brush your teeth. Then I'll read to you in Grace's room, since she'll be going to bed first."

When the kids were ready, we settled ourselves on Grace's bed in a row. I read *The Snowy Day* first and Henry said he wished New York would get more snow. Grace said she wished the snow would stay white. (In New York, the snow turns slushy gray and brown almost as soon as it falls.)

Then we read *The Owl and the Pussycat* and Grace tried to recite the poem along with me, but she kept getting the words wrong. She called the runcible spoon a "crunchable spoon," and five-pound note a "five-pound goat." She made Henry giggle.

When the stories were finished, Henry and I said good night to Grace, and she snuggled under her covers. Then she raised her arms for a hug.

"Good night, Grace," I said softly as Henry and I left the room.

I closed her door, taking a long look at her walls as I did so. They were covered with her drawings and paintings.

Then I walked Henry to his room and we read one more book together, *Angus and the Ducks*, before Henry went to bed, too. And as I left Henry's room, I also took a long look at his walls. I felt almost as if I might not see those walls again.

Why did I feel that way?

With Grace and Henry safely in bed, I sat down in the Walkers' living room. My schoolbooks were in a stack on the coffee table. I flipped through them. I had a ton of homework to catch up on, but I knew I wouldn't be able to concentrate.

I closed the books and leaned back against the couch to think. The first things that came to my mind were Judy's words from the day before. "Crying shame," she'd said about the divorce. What had she meant? If she were being sarcastic, maybe she'd had a right. After all, she had no family, no job, not even a home. My parents were getting a divorce; that was all. It sort of put things in perspective. I was not nearly in such bad shape as Judy was.

Still, I did have problems. Soon I was going to have to make some big decisions. If Mom left New York, could I really go with her? Could I leave New York again? How could I leave behind everything I love? I'd have to leave Laine, Grace, Henry, and the city it-self — and I truly ♡ New York. Every time I have to leave it, I have a hard time. Moving to Stoneybrook had been difficult and I'd been glad to get back. Even going to Camp Mohawk for two weeks had been hard. I'd been glad to get back then, too.

On the other hand, I had more friends in Stoneybrook than I did in New York. In New York I hung around with Laine and her friends at school, but Laine's friends really were *her* friends. Much more hers than mine. I always felt on the edges of things with Laine's crowd. In Stoneybrook, I was one of the coolest kids around, but not in New York. In New York, I had a lot of competition for the Queen of Cool. And I would never win the crown.

I knew that I was heading for a bad time in my life, a time when I'd have to adjust to a lot of things. Would that adjustment be easier in a nice safe place like Stoneybrook, where I was surrounded by good friends? Probably.

On the other hand, how could I leave New

York for a second time? How could I leave Bloomingdale's and Broadway and shopping and The Last Wound-Up and great movie theaters and even greater restaurants, like the Hard Rock Cafe? Would I be bored silly in Stoneybrook, with only Washington Mall for entertainment? Maybe.

But I was missing two big pieces to the puzzle. If I went to Stoneybrook, I would have to leave my dad. How could I do that? If I stayed in New York, I would have to leave my mom. How could I do *that*? I might be mad at them now, but I still loved them. A lot.

Furthermore, I bet Dad would be hurt if I chose to live with Mom, and I bet Mom would be hurt if I chose to live with Dad. They'd said the decision was up to me, which was nice, but someone — Mom or Dad — was going to get hurt. And I was going to be the cause of the pain.

Maybe I could arrange to live with one parent during the school week when we wouldn't see each other much anyway, and the other parent all the rest of the time. That would work if Mom didn't move too far away. But what if she moved to Maine or someplace?

It was too much to think about.

I guess that was why Dawn had recommended taking one step at a time.

However, I wouldn't have any problems at all if my parents were not getting a divorce. Now that was something to think about.

Maybe, just maybe, I could do what that so-called marriage counselor hadn't been able to do. Maybe I could get my parents to quit thinking about a divorce and make them remember "till death do us part."

It was certainly worth a try.

All I needed were a few good ideas and a little romance.

I took a piece of paper out of my notebook and began scribbling away — not at homework, but at a list of ideas. By the time the Walkers came home, I had filled up nearly a page. I could hardly wait to try my ideas!

I was sure I could get my parents together again. They probably just needed encouragement from someone who knew them. And who was the "marriage" counselor? A stranger, that's who.

But I was Stacey McGill, their daughter.

And if anyone could fix things up for them, I could.

CHAPTER 9

That next week was a busy one.

On Saturday afternoon, while my parents were seeing their lawyers, I went to a theater and bought three tickets (with baby-sitting money) to a movie I knew we all wanted to see. My plan was to wait until almost the last minute to give Mom and Dad the tickets, to ensure that we wouldn't be able to find three seats in a row once we got to the theater. Then I'd insist that my parents sit together while I found a single seat.

But when I gave them the tickets, Dad said, "Stacey, what a nice surprise, but I plan to spend the evening combing the paper for apartment ads. Why don't you and your mom take Laine instead?"

So we did, and anyway we found three seats together.

* * *

On Sunday, I suggested a carriage ride through Central Park. This was particularly meaningful, since years ago Dad had proposed to Mom in one of those carriages. My new plan was to wait until my parents had already climbed into the carriage, and then say, "Uh-oh! I forgot to give myself my insulin. You guys go on without me."

But we never even made it to Central Park. Mom liked the idea, but this time *she* was busy reading the real estate section of the paper and didn't want to leave the apartment.

On Monday when I got home from school I was delighted to find Mom out for the afternoon. Time for plan number three. I put our card table in the middle of the living room, covered it with a white tablecloth, set it for a romantic dinner for two, and cooked up a meal of chicken and vegetables. I even made two ice-cream parfaits for dessert. When my parents came home, I would tell them that I'd been invited to Laine's for dinner, and leave them to the romance. But Dad didn't come home. He phoned to say that he was going to spend the evening apartment-hunting and then sleep at his office. (He does that sometimes. There's a couch in his office and he keeps a clean suit hanging behind the door.)

So Mom and I ate the dinner (but I saved the second parfait for Dad).

On Tuesday I was out of ideas. Ditto on Wednesday.

But by Thursday I was rolling again. I slipped each of my parents a note written on the official paper of my school, saying that I was behind in my work and that my guidance counselor wanted to meet them for dinner at the Silver Spur, a restaurant in our neighborhood. Unfortunately, Mom and Dad both smelled a trick and called the guidance counselor. Why did they have to be so smart? If they'd just followed directions, they would have had a nice, romantic dinner together and called off the divorce. Instead, I got in trouble with Mom, Dad, *and* my counselor, and was also given three weeks in which to catch up on my homework. I guessed the special treatment was over.

So much for romance.

On Saturday morning, Mom unexpectedly announced, "Stacey, I'm going to drive up to Stoneybrook today to house-hunt." Then she added, "Why don't you come with me?"

I thought and thought. I didn't really want to leave the city, and Laine had said something about going to a play that night. On the other hand, I wanted to see Claud and the other members of the BSC. And if Mom was going to buy a house in Stoneybrook, I wanted to have some say in her choice. I didn't want to end up with, like, some dinky, falling-apart, olive-green house in a teeny yard with no grass.

"Okay," I said nonchalantly to Mom. "I'll go with you."

I barely had time to phone Laine and tell her I wouldn't be able to go to the play. Mom was waiting for me, holding the door to the apartment open as I hung up, so I couldn't even call Claudia. Oh, well. I would just surprise her.

And, boy, did I surprise her! As we were driving to Stoneybrook, Mom said, "Honey? Would you like to invite Claudia to house-hunt with us?"

"Sure!" I cried. "Oh, she'll *die* of excitement!"

"Well, don't let her," said Mom with a smile. "And remind her that we're not *sure* we'll be moving here. We're just checking out the real estate. I've heard it's a buyer's market, but I want to see for myself."

I didn't know what a buyer's market was and I didn't care. I was too busy imagining pulling into the Kishis' driveway, running up their front walk, ringing the bell, and giving Claudia a heart attack when she answered it. It never occurred to me that the Kishis might not be at home, or that Janine or Mr. or Mrs. Kishi might answer the door.

And it didn't matter, because things went just as I'd imagined. We arrived in Stoneybrook, Mom stopped to buy a paper and to call a real estate agent, agreed on a place to meet the agent, and then we pulled into the Kishis' driveway. I ran up their walk, rang the bell, Claud answered the door, and for a second, I thought she really was going to have a heart attack.

At last she managed to gasp out, *"Stacey?"*

I giggled. "Yup. It's me."

Claud threw the storm door open and we hugged and hugged.

"What are you doing here? How come you didn't call first?" asked Claud.

"It was spur of the moment," I replied. "Mom didn't give me a chance. She was in such a hurry to get here and start house-hunting. We're supposed to meet an agent in fifteen minutes. Want to come look at houses with us?"

"Are you kidding? Of course I do!"

Claud had to find her father, though, explain what was going on, and show him that my mom really was parked in the driveway. Then she jumped into the backseat with me.

"So you're actually moving back to Stoneybrook?" she cried. "This is awesome. Totally awesome!"

Mom smiled. "It isn't definite yet, Claudia." She pulled into the street and turned right. "But it's certainly *my* first choice for a place to live."

Claud looked at me with raised eyebrows, meaning, "And you? This is your first choice, too, isn't it?"

But I just shook my head at her. We could discuss that some other time — when Mom wasn't in earshot.

"Okay," said my mother, "we're supposed to meet this agent — her name is Ms. Keller — at Forty-two twenty-one Rosedale."

"Oh, I know where Rosedale is, Mrs. McGill," said Claudia, and she directed us there.

We found the address without any trouble,

and also found Ms. Keller waiting in the driveway.

Mom and Ms. Keller shook hands, and Mom began explaining why we were moving and what she was looking for in a house, while Claud and I gazed suspiciously at 4221 Rosedale. It was not my olive-green nightmare house, but it wasn't any dream house, either.

"It's kind of small," said Claudia tactfully. (The place was the size of a bird feeder.)

"There aren't any trees in the yard, either," I pointed out. There was grass, though, so it wasn't a total loss.

Just then we heard Ms. Keller say brightly to Mom, "Well, let's take a look inside, shall we?"

The four of us picked our way up the crumbling walk to the front door. I pulled Mom aside and whispered, "Can't we afford something nicer?"

Mom's cryptic answer was, "We're on a tight budget."

Tight budget or not, nobody liked the inside of 4221 Rosedale any better than the outside. Even Ms. Keller. I could tell. Faucets dripped, the kitchen looked like it would have to be sandblasted before it could even be cleaned, and three of the rooms were painted purple, ceilings and all.

Mom gave Ms. Keller a tiny smile. "What else do you have in our price range?" she asked.

"A little house on Burnt Hill Road," Ms. Keller replied.

"Burnt Hill Road. That's where Dawn lives!" Claudia cried.

We got back in our car and followed Ms. Keller to the second house. It wasn't near Dawn's, and it wasn't as nice, either. The front porch was going to need replacing, the roof needed reshingling, and the house was pink. We'd have to repaint it.

"I wish we could move back to our old house," I said wistfully, "but Jessi's in it."

"Anyway, it's out of our price range," whispered Mom.

The next house Ms. Keller showed us wasn't bad at all — but it was next door to an olive-green, grassless nightmare house. Littering the bare yard were two broken-down cars, a refrigerator with no door, three rusty bicycles, and a lot of tools I couldn't identify.

Claudia pulled me aside. "That place gets worse at Christmastime," she told me conspiratorially. "The owners outline the *entire house* — windows, doors, everything — with colored lights. They put a mechanical Santa on the chimney, and all day and all night he waves one arm back and forth and goes, 'Ho-ho-ho. Ho-ho-ho.' They set wooden carolers in the yard and elves on the front steps, and they shine a spotlight onto the roof where they put a Rudolph with a blinking red nose."

"Mom," I said, "I could not live next door to reindeer and a refrigerator."

"I agree," Mom replied. "Anything else, Ms. Keller?"

The real estate agent consulted a book. "We-ell," she said after a few moments, "there is something bigger in your price range and in a nicer neighborhood, but — "

"Let's see it," interrupted Mom.

So we drove to a house not far from the one we'd just seen. And as soon as we'd gotten out of the car, Claudia cried, "I know this house! It's right behind Mallory's! Look through the backyard, Stacey. See? There's the back of the Pikes' house."

I looked. I could even see the triplets fooling around with a bat and ball.

"I thought someone lived here," Claud said

to Ms. Keller. Then she whispered to me, "The people were really weird and the Pike kids used to spy on them."

"That couple moved out awhile ago," Ms. Keller told us.

"Gosh, they didn't stay very long," mused Claudia.

From the outside, the house didn't look bad. A little weird, maybe, but in pretty good shape except for a few small problems like a loose brick in the front steps and a crooked shutter.

"How old is the house?" Mom asked, as Ms. Keller unlocked the front door.

"Turn of the century. Actually, probably a little older. Eighteen-eighties."

"Eighteen-eighty," I whispered to Claud. "Pretty old."

We stepped into a dark hallway. The house smelled musty, the air was stale, and a thin layer of dust covered everything.

"It has the typical old-house problems, but with just a little work, you can see that it would be a lovely home. Not too big, not too small, and plenty of attractive old features." Ms. Keller showed us a bathtub resting on claw feet, a bedroom with dormer windows, and a kitchen with appliances that appeared to be about a thousand years old.

"They all work, though," Ms. Keller informed us. Then she added, "At least for the time being."

Mom looked at me. I shrugged. It *was* kind of a neat house, but still . . .

"I'll give you my answer within a week," Mom told the agent.

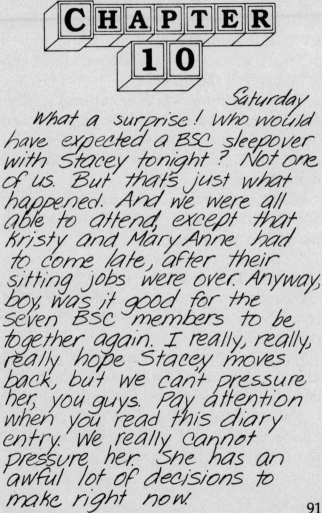

CHAPTER 10

Saturday

What a surprise! Who would have expected a BSC sleepover with Stacey tonight? Not one of us. But that's just what happened. And we were all able to attend, except that Kristy and Mary Anne had to come late, after their sitting jobs were over. Anyway, boy, was it good for the seven BSC members to be together again. I really, really, really hope Stacey moves back, but we can't pressure her, you guys. Pay attention when you read this diary entry. We really cannot pressure her. She has an awful lot of decisions to make right now.

91

Dawn was on the phone with her brother Jeff when Claudia and I called her from the Kishis' house. Since the Schafers have call-waiting, Dawn put Jeff on hold and spoke to us for a few moments.

"You'll never guess where I am," I told her.

"Where?" asked Dawn.

"In Stoneybrook. I'm over at Claud's. Mom and I were up here house-hunting today, and Mom drove back to New York, but she said I could spend the night here and take the train home tomorrow."

Claud took the phone from me then and added, "BSC slumber party at my house tonight. Can you come?"

"Sure!" exclaimed Dawn.

"Great. Be here around seven."

Dawn had to get back to Jeff then, so Claud and I hung up and began calling the other club members.

What an unexpected weekend this had turned out to be. First house-hunting, and now a slumber party, just like in the old days! I couldn't believe Mom had let me stay in Connecticut. (But I was happy knowing I would return to New York the next day.)

* * *

Promptly at seven o'clock, the Kishis' bell rang. "That must be Dawn," said Claud. "She is always exactly on time. See? My digital clock says seven on the nose."

It was Dawn at the door. She was quickly followed by Jessi and Mal. The five of us settled ourselves in Claud's room with hoagies and salad. We had a real feast. Then Claud and Mal attacked a package of Oreos (hidden in the closet), Jessi delicately took a single Oreo (she watches her weight to stay in shape for dancing), and Dawn and I passed up the junk food. We braided each other's hair instead.

At eight-thirty the Kishis' bell rang again, and soon we heard feet pounding on the stairs.

"Kristy's here!" said Claud, giggling.

The rest of us smiled. No one else can thunder up a flight of stairs quite the way Kristy can.

"Hi!" cried Kristy. "Hi, you guys! Hi, Stacey!" Kristy is not much of a hugger, but she opened her arms and we hugged anyway. "I'm so glad to see you!" she said. "Did you find a decent house? I'm starved."

Kristy can be hard to keep up with.

"You're *starved*?" said Claud. "You were sitting at the Rodowskys' at dinnertime. Didn't you eat there?"

"I ate part of a hot dog when I fed the boys, but that was it. I was so busy cleaning up after Jackie that I didn't have time to eat anything else."

I sat back down on the bed with Dawn and we began working on each other's hair again, while Jessi and Mal experimented with Claudia's makeup and nail polish.

"What did Jackie do tonight?" I couldn't resist asking.

"Squirted his hot dog across the kitchen the second he bit into it — " Kristy began, grinning.

"He bit into the kitchen?" said Dawn.

"No, the *hot* dog!"

"The hot dog bit into the kitchen?"

We all started laughing.

See? This is what I love about my friends up here. They're so . . . natural. They don't spend every second of their lives trying to impress each other. Sure, they talk about boys sometimes, and they care about how they look (well, some of them do), but those things aren't the focus of their lives. With my friends in New York (except for Laine) *all* they do is talk about who's dating whom, where they went, what they ate, and what they wore. Or who's going skiing in Aspen, or who'll get the best tan in Bermuda over spring vacation.

"Do you want something to eat?" Claudia asked Kristy.

"*Any*thing," she replied desperately.

"There's half a hoagie left over," said Claud. "I'll go get it for you."

Claudia left the room, and Kristy sat in her favorite place, the director's chair. She didn't bother with the visor, though, since we weren't having a meeting.

A few moments later, Claud returned with not only the hoagie, but Mary Anne.

Another happy reunion followed, and then the seven of us got down to serious slumber-party business. First, we took Mal and Jessi's lead, and all painted our nails. I painted my fingernails with sparkly pink polish. Then I painted my toenails with clear pink polish and added a green dot in the center of each one.

"Who's going to see your toes?" asked Kristy, who would only go so far as to paint her fingernails with clear polish.

"Me," I replied. "I like to look good for myself."

Dawn grinned. "You're the most important person to look good for," she informed us. "I always dress to please myself."

"Speaking of that," said Kristy, "you know what Alan Gray wore to school last Wednesday?"

"Oh, lord," moaned Claud, burying her face in her hands, apparently remembering.

"What? What?" I asked.

"A hat with an alligator on top of it, and when he pulled this string, the alligator's mouth opened and closed, and its tail waved back and forth."

We were laughing again. That's another thing I love about these friends. We laugh a lot. We've done our share of crying together and being scared together, but mostly when I think of us as a group, I think of the laughter.

"How is old Alan Gray?" I asked. Alan is the bane of Kristy's existence. He'd like her for his girlfriend, but he's *so* immature. Besides, Kristy likes Bart Taylor, the coach of Bart's Bashers.

"Don't ask," was Kristy's reply.

"Okay. Let me try another question. How's Emily?"

Immediately, Kristy softened. She just loves her new little sister, I can tell.

"I've got pictures!" exclaimed Kristy. "I almost forgot. I brought them over just for you. I can't believe I nearly left them in my knapsack all night."

The seven BSC members crowded together on Claudia's bed.

"See? There's Emily all dressed up to go see Watson's parents. And there she is playing peek-a-boo with Nannie." (Nannie is Kristy's grandmother, her mother's mother, who lives at the Brewer mansion and helps take care of the kids and the house.) "Oh," Kristy went on, "and there's Emily dressing up in my clothes. Look, my Kristy's Krushers T-shirt is like a dress on her!"

Kristy had about a hundred photos of Emily Michelle. Well, not really, but it took us awhile to look through them. When we were done, we changed into our nightgowns, spread sleeping bags on the floor of Claud's room, crawled inside them, and began to gossip. Every now and then, somebody would get up, go into the bathroom, brush her teeth, return to her sleeping bag, and drift off to sleep.

At last, only Claud and I were awake. The lights were off in her room, but each of us knew the other wasn't asleep yet.

"Stace?" whispered Claud.

"Yeah?"

"Remember how awful it was when you first found out you were moving back to New York?"

"Yeah."

"We tried to figure out a way for you to stay here."

"Yeah."

"And I said you were my first and only best friend."

"I remember."

"Well, you still are. You always will be. Whether you live here or in New York or — or in Nepal."

"Nepal!?" We put our hands over our mouths to muffle our giggling. "Thanks, Claud," I said. "You know what? I feel like you're my sister."

I fell asleep happy — and guilty. Because for all the fun I was having, and as close as I felt to Claud and my other friends, I couldn't wait to get back to New York the next day.

New York, I admitted to myself, was Home.

CHAPTER 11

Back to New York City, back Home. I was in school again. I hung around with Laine. I stepped gingerly around our group of friends at school. I baby-sat for Grace and Henry. I watched Mom and Dad read the real estate pages of the paper.

And I missed Stoneybrook. How could that be? New York was Home, but all I could think of was Connecticut, Claud, and the BSC.

One night Dad came home late to announce that he'd found an apartment. Mom and I were in the kitchen. Supper was over and we were drinking tea. I was doing math homework (my easiest subject), and Mom was making a list of pros and cons about the house in Stoneybrook. She couldn't make up her mind about it, and I wasn't being much help. I had decided to stop saying anything about where I wanted to live or whom I wanted to live with.

This was a feeble effort at keeping Mom and Dad together. I thought maybe I could be uncooperative enough to make them rethink the stupid divorce thing.

I was wrong.

Dad strode into the kitchen, smiling. "I found a place, Stacey," he said, as if Mom weren't sitting just three feet away from him. "You'll love it, I know. It's in an older, smaller building, it has lots of charm, and just like I promised, there are two bedrooms — one for me, one for you. Here take a look at the ad."

Dad handed me a miniscule piece of paper that he'd cut out of *The New York Times*.

I frowned at it. *Wb fp. So exp. Pre-war bldg. Brk wls.* I looked at Dad. "Woodbug fup? So expee? Pre-war bulldog? Bark wools? Where are you going to live? In Wonderland?"

Dad laughed. "No. That means a wood-burning fireplace, southern exposure — in other words, lots of sunlight — and a pre-war building with several brick walls. Believe me, you've never seen anything like it."

"And you've already taken it?" asked Mom in a strange voice.

"Yup. Well, I've paid two months' rent. I just have to sign a few papers tomorrow."

"Where's the apartment, Dad?" I asked.

100

"The East Sixties. East Sixty-fifth Street, to be exact."

"But I've never lived on the East Side," I said.

"Well, you can experience it now," Dad replied.

A horrible expression crossed Mom's face. Mine, too, but for a different reason.

"You want to live with your father, Stacey?" cried Mom, at the same time I said, "You mean you're really, really going through with it? You guys are really getting divorced?"

For a moment, no one knew what to say. Then we all began talking at once.

Dad said, "You knew our decision was final, Anastasia."

Mom said, "I thought you'd want to go back to Stoneybrook, Stacey."

I said, "I thought I could live wherever I wanted. You said that was up to me. Besides, I didn't say I was going to live with Dad, just that I've never lived on the East Side."

Then Dad said, "East Sixty-fifth Street is just inches away from Bloomingdale's."

And Mom said, "Don't bribe her. That's not fair."

And I said, "I thought this was just a phase you two were going through."

And Mom said, "Take your insulin, Stacey."

And Dad said, "Don't hound her."

And I said, "I hate you both," and ran to my room and slammed the door.

The next day was Saturday. Dad went to a real estate office to sign some papers, and then to a gigantic hardware store that carries everything from nuts and bolts to refrigerator magnets. He said he needed some things for his new pad.

His new *pad*. He actually said that.

I stayed at home with Mom, feeling horribly guilty about those words that had slipped out of my mouth the night before: "I've never lived on the East Side."

I sat in the kitchen with her again while she looked at the paper. I was trying to write an English composition (the teacher had said to write about what you know, so I was writing about parents who can't keep their marriage vows), but concentrating was difficult with Mom on the phone every two seconds.

It was especially difficult when I heard her say, "Hello, Ms. Keller?"

Right away, my ears perked up.

"This is Mrs. McGill," Mom went on. "Yes. . . . Right. . . . Well, I know it's been a week, and I'm calling to say that I just can't make up my mind about the house. It is a lovely old place, but it will probably be expensive to keep up, and . . . Well, I know. . . . I know. So I wanted to tell you that I guess you better start showing the house again. If I decide I want it, I'll call to find out if it's still available, and if it isn't, I'll understand. . . . Okay. . . . Yes. . . . All right. Thank you. Good-bye."

"What did Ms. Keller say?" I asked.

"That the house'll probably be snapped up in a second."

"Oh."

My mother returned to the paper.

"Mom?"

"Yes, honey?"

"How come you can't make up your mind about the house in Stoneybrook?"

"I guess because it's too big for one person. If I knew what *you* wanted to do — I mean, where you wanted to live — "

"So get a smaller house," I said. "One with just two bedrooms. The old house has four."

"I didn't see any *nice* smaller houses."

"Oh, yeah." I remembered the refrigerator and the reindeer.

"I think I'll look on Long Island," said Mom, rattling the paper as she turned pages.

Long Island? When I visited her there, I wouldn't know anybody. She had to move to Stoneybrook, I thought.

I flipped to the back of my composition book and tore out a fresh page. Then I made a list of pros and cons. One list was for staying in New York. The other list was for leaving New York and going back to Connecticut. Here is what my page looked like:

New York	Stoneybrook
I love it.	It's OK.
A zillion things to do here.	Not much to do.
I can always <u>visit</u> Stoneybrook.	I can always <u>visit</u> New York.
Laine.	Claudia, Kristy, Mary Anne, Dawn, Jessi, Mal.
Henry and Grace.	Charlotte.
Baby-sitting.	The Baby-sitters Club.
I love Dad.	I love Mom, and I'm very close to her.
I'd get to be with Dad.	Mom is around more than Dad is.
I'd get to know Dad better.	Mom understands me better than Dad does.

104

If Dad wanted to go away for the weekend, he <u>might</u> let me stay alone. (Or he might not)	If Mom wanted to go away for the weekend, I'd have tons of friends to stay with.
I go to a good school in New York.	I like Stoneybrook Middle School better than my school in New York.
Maybe I would like the East Side better than the West Side.	I know what I'm getting into when I move to Stoneybrook.
The kids here are very sophisticated.	There's no peer pressure with my friends in Stoneybrook.

I took a look at my list. I didn't have to look at it very long to see the decision I was going to make.

"Mom?" I said. "Can you call Ms. Keller back right now?"

"Sure. But why?"

"Just to make sure no one snapped up the house in the last fifteen minutes."

Mom gave me a questioning look but dialed the phone anyway. She spoke briefly to Ms. Keller, then cupped her hand over the phone and raised her eyebrows at me.

I took a deep breath. "Ask her if you and I can move into it."

Mom's eyes filled with tears, and in a wavery voice, she told Ms. Keller that she'd take the house after all. Then they began talking business, and I tuned out. All I could think of was what I would tell my father when he came home.

Dad returned late that afternoon. He'd been putting shelf paper in the kitchen cabinets of his new pad.

"Dad," I said, "I have to talk to you. In private. Can we go to my room?"

"Of course, honey."

Dad followed me to my room and sat next to me on the bed. How, I wondered, could I possibly say what I had to say? My father and I love each other, and now I was going to hurt him. He had stayed with me during hospital visits. He had helped me learn to give myself insulin injections. He had bought me dolls and dresses and taken me to my first Broadway play — *Annie*.

"Dad," I began, already knowing I was going to cry, "I made a decision today. I'm going to Stoneybrook with Mom. She took the house we found last week."

My father just nodded. I don't know whether he'd expected the news or not.

"You said it was up to me," I whispered.

Dad nodded again. His Adam's apple was moving up and down.

"I knew it. I knew I'd hurt you," I said.

"Oh, Stacey. I'm, well, I guess I am a little hurt," Dad told me. "I'd be lying if I said I wasn't. But I'm not angry. I'm just going to miss you an awful lot. That's all."

"I'll visit," I promised him, wiping away the tears that were dripping down my cheeks. "Every other weekend. Or maybe all summer. We'll work something out."

"I know we will."

I handed Dad a Kleenex and took one for myself. Then we hugged each other and cried and cried.

CHAPTER 12

"Hey, Mom!" I shouted. "We need more packing cartons!"

"Run to Gristede's," Mom called from the living room. "See if they have any. Sometimes they have the ones with tops."

Run to Gristede's. Run to Gristede's. If I had a dollar for every time I'd been to that grocery store asking for cartons, I'd never need to baby-sit again in my life.

It was two weeks after I'd made my decision. The three of us would be moving in just one week. I felt as if all I'd done during the past two years was pack. And it wasn't over. When Mom and I reached Stoneybrook, we'd have to *un*pack.

I thought about that as I put on my jacket and left our apartment, heading for Gristede's.

"Have fun and be careful!" called Mom.

"You, too!" I replied.

The elevator and I plummeted to the lobby, and I walked outside. I'd given Laine the news about our move not long after I'd told Dad. Laine had cried, too, which had made me start crying again.

"You *can't* move," she'd wailed. "What'll I do without you?"

"The same things you did when I moved to Stoneybrook the first time. Write to me. Call me. We'll run up huge phone bills."

"It won't be the same."

"I know. But you have Allison and Jean and everyone."

"They're not you."

I sighed. "I'm going to miss you, too," I said, "in case you'd forgotten."

That was when the tears started.

So I decided to give myself a break. I called someone who would be happy to hear the news. Claudia.

"Oh, my lord. Oh, my *lord!*" she shrieked. "You're really coming *back?*" And then *Claud* began to cry.

They were tears of happiness, of course, but nevertheless, they were more tears, and I couldn't help crying again, too. At that rate, I thought, my whole head would dry up.

At Gristede's, I stepped up to the manager's

office and peered through her little window. I'd been in the store so often looking for boxes that the manager, Miss Antonio, and I knew each other, although we did not like each other. I found Miss Antonio trying on a new hat. Three of the cashiers were crowded into the booth with her, giving her advice on how to wear it.

"Ahem." I drummed my fingers on the ledge under the window.

"Turn it around a little," one of the cashiers suggested to Miss Antonio. (Her name tag read "Anita.")

"Like this?" Miss Antonio swung the brim around.

"No, more like this," said Anita, adjusting the hat.

"Ahem," I said again.

"And tilt it up," added Anita.

Miss Antonio tilted it.

I banged my fist on the bell at the window. *DING, DING, DING!*

Miss Antonio and her friends looked up in annoyance.

"Oh, it's you," said Miss Antonio. "There are some boxes in the back. You can go get 'em yourself."

"Thank you *so* much for your attention and courtesy," I replied.

The next time we needed cartons, Mom could get them.

I found five cartons (without lids, unfortunately), nested them inside one another, and walked them home. On the way, I passed Judy. I could see that she was not in one of her good moods, but I stopped and said, "Hey, Judy, next week I'm moving to Connecticut with my mom."

Judy stared at me for a moment. Then she shrieked, "The heads of corporations are liars! Do you hear me?" (They could hear her in Toledo.) "They're corrupting our country with their plastic and their Campbell's soup and . . ."

Judy's voice trailed after me as I headed for home.

When I reached my apartment, I could hear Mom and Dad arguing. Even so, I yelled over their noise, "I was careful and I had a *ton* of fun. Next time one of you can go have fun with Miss Antonio. Be sure to admire her hat."

Mom and Dad probably thought I was crazy, but they went right back to their arguing without asking me what I was talking about. So I left three of the cartons in the living room and took the others to my bedroom.

I closed the door.

But I could still hear Mom say, "The crystal vase? You can't have the crystal vase. That was a present from Donna and Stewart. Donna's one of my best friends."

"And Stew is one of *my* best friends," Dad countered loudly.

It wasn't easy dividing up a houseful of furniture and memories. Mom and Dad had been fighting constantly over who got what. The biggest fights were over items of sentimental value, such as photograph albums and wedding gifts. Naturally, they both wanted all those things.

I turned on my tape deck and put the headphones on to drown out the arguing. I concentrated on my own packing. Most of my things were going to Connecticut, of course, but I was sending a few things to Dad's apartment. I didn't want a totally bare room there, and besides, the less I had to pack when I visited him, the better. Some clothes, some makeup, some books, some tapes, my Walkman, some posters, and a few other things were going to Dad's. The rest was going to our new house in Stoneybrook.

112

I looked around my half-empty room.

I lifted the headphones tentatively — just in time to hear Mom say, "You may *not* have that painting. I bought it myself!"

"With *my* money!" shouted Dad.

I put the headphones back on in a hurry.

Then I burst into tears for about the zillionth time.

Thursday night. I was baby-sitting for Henry and Grace. It would be my last time. Forty-eight hours from then I would be back in Stoneybrook.

I knew that Mr. and Mrs. Walker had explained to Henry and Grace that I was moving, but I wasn't sure that they understood what that meant.

Sure enough, as soon as the Walkers left and Grace had stopped crying, Henry said, "Mommy and Daddy said you can't baby-sit us anymore."

I nodded. "That's right."

"How come?"

It was seven-thirty. Henry and Grace were in their pajamas (Grace's had feet, Henry's didn't), and they were ready for bed. I sat the kids down on the living room couch, one on either side of me, and tried to explain. "See,"

113

I began, putting an arm around each of them, "my mom and dad don't want to live together anymore, so they're each moving to a new home. I decided to live with my mom, and she's going to live in a faraway place called Connecticut."

"Why don't your mommy and daddy want to live together anymore?" asked Grace.

"Because they fight all the time," I told her. "They stopped being in love with each other."

Henry looked alarmed. "Tonight our mommy and daddy had a fight," he said. "Mommy went, 'Where on earth are our keys? You never put them away in the same place.' And Daddy went, 'I just *told* you they're on the bookshelf.' And Mommy went, 'Well, I guess I didn't hear you.'"

"Oh, but Henry, that was just a little argument," I assured him. "People argue all the time. My parents' fights were big. They were *huge*. Mom and Dad didn't even want to be in the same room together. So they're getting a divorce. Your parents are not getting a divorce."

"Yeah," said Grace. "This morning Mommy said to Daddy, 'I love you,' and Daddy said, 'I love you, too.' Then they kissed."

I smiled. "That's nice. You guys don't have a thing to worry about."

I walked the kids into Grace's bedroom, where we read *Millions of Cats*. Then I tucked her in, said good night to her, and walked Henry to *his* bedroom, where we read *Outside Over There*.

"I'll see you on Saturday before we leave," I told him. "Your family's coming to my apartment to say good-bye. Okay?"

"Okay."

" 'Night, Henry."

" 'Night, Stacey. I love you."

"I love you, too."

I sat in the Walkers' living room with my math book open in front of me. Would Henry and Grace find a new sitter that they liked? Would they find one they liked as much as me? Part of me hoped so — and part of me didn't, because I wanted to be somebody's special baby-sitter. But I knew I'd be sitting for Charlotte Johanssen soon again anyway. So I felt better.

CHAPTER 13

On Saturday morning I woke up with a jolt. Usually I only wake up with a jolt when the alarm clock rings. This time, no alarm went off — except for the one in my brain, which was shouting, "MOVING DAY!"

Oh, no. Please. Not that, I thought. I turned onto my stomach, put the pillow over my head, and tried to drown out reality. Moving was bad enough, but that day was also the true beginning of my parents' divorce. I would officially become a divorced kid. I would join the ranks of Dawn and Kristy, of Keith, Shayla, and Caitlin.

"Stace!" called my father from the hallway. "Up and at 'em!"

When had he come over? What time was it? Later than I thought, apparently. Dad had been sleeping at his new pad ever since his new bed had arrived. But he'd promised to come over early that last morning to help with the movers and to see me off. (I noticed he'd said see *me* off, not *us* off. I guessed Mom didn't count too much anymore.)

"Okay!" I called to Dad.

I removed the pillow from my head, rolled over, and peered at my alarm clock. It, some clothes, and my furniture were the only things in my room. Everything else had been packed into cartons. Even the rug had been rolled up.

"Eight forty-five!" I said aloud. "Yikes!"

The movers were supposed to arrive at ten. And before that, Laine and the Walkers were coming over. I leaped out of bed.

I bet I set a showering and dressing record that morning. By five after nine I was heading to the kitchen for breakfast.

That was when one of the doormen buzzed from downstairs.

"Oh, no! The movers can't be here already!" I cried.

"Don't worry," said Dad, who was sorting out cartons in the living room, making a His pile and a Hers pile. "Movers are never early. It's a law. It may even be written in the Constitution."

I laughed. My father often makes me laugh. I would miss that.

I pressed the Talk button on our intercom. "Yes?" I said.

"Laine's on her way up," Isaac told me. He would always let Laine come up without bothering to ask me if she could. It saved time. Usually he didn't even call to let me know she was coming.

"Thanks," I replied, just as the doorbell rang.

I ran to answer it. When I opened the door, there stood Laine, her arms full. She was carrying a big grocery bag.

"Oh, no," I said. "I hope that's not something we have to pack."

Laine grinned as she stepped inside and I closed the door behind her. "You can pack it into yourselves. It's breakfast," she told me.

"Breakfast?"

"One last famous New York breakfast — bagels, lox, cream cheese, and orange juice. Oh, and coffee for your parents. I figured the coffee maker and everything would be packed."

"Laine, I love you!" I cried. "This is terrific." I sniffled.

"You aren't going to cry again, are you?" asked Laine.

"No," I said, even though I'd been ready to

really let loose. I still couldn't believe what was happening to me that day.

Laine handed me the bag and we took it into the kitchen. I peeked inside.

"Oh! Paper plates! And plastic spoons and knives! You thought of everything," I exclaimed. "Dad! Mom! Come here and see what Laine brought!"

My parents appeared in the kitchen a few moments later. They took a look at the spread, including the cups of steaming coffee, and the little packages of sugar and the containers of cream.

I leaned over to Laine and whispered, "I bet Mom's going to say, 'Laine, you shouldn't have!' "

"Laine, you shouldn't have!" cried Mom.

Laine and I burst into giggles.

Mom and Dad smiled. "What is it?" asked Dad. "A private joke?"

"Yeah," I said. I gave Laine a sideways glance and we started laughing again. Boy, am I going to miss you, I thought.

To keep from crying, I handed out paper plates, and the four of us set to work slicing bagels in half, spreading cream cheese on them, and layering the lox on top of the cream cheese.

"Mmm," I said, relishing the first bite. "This is heaven."

We sat down at the table. I looked around at Mom and Dad and Laine. We could be a family, I thought. Mom and Dad could be my nondivorced parents and Laine could be my sister. Then I thought, Maybe we are a family anyway. Maybe you don't have to be blood relatives to be family.

"This was awfully nice of you, Laine," said my father.

"Well," Laine replied, "I thought Stacey and Mrs. McGill should have one final, authentic, New York breakfast before they left for the wilderness."

"The wilderness!" I started laughing again.

"We *can* get bagels in Connecticut," Mom pointed out, smiling.

"But they're kind of like hockey pucks, remember?" I said.

Mom nodded. Then she looked at her watch. "Oh, goodness! Just half an hour until the movers are supposed to be here! We better get — "

" — cracking," my father finished for her.

And I thought, How can they get divorced? They still finish each other's sentences. Then something awful occurred to me. Actually, several things. I don't know why I hadn't thought of them before.

"Dad!" I cried. "You don't know how to cook . . . do you? And Mom, how are we going to take care of our lawn? Neither one of us has ever mowed one before. And Dad, do you know that you're supposed to wash white clothes in hot water and colored clothes in — "

"Honey, calm down," said Dad. "Everything will be okay."

I was about to protest when the doorbell rang.

"I can't believe Isaac didn't announce the movers," exclaimed Mom, flying out of her chair.

"Relax," I told her. "I think it's the Walkers. They want to say good-bye." I ran to the door. Before I opened it, I called, "Hello?" (In New York, you can't be too careful.)

"It's us! It's us!" shouted Henry's voice.

I let the Walkers inside while Laine and my parents gathered in the living room.

"Stacey?" Grace whispered. She was hugging my legs and leaning back to look up at me.

"Yes?" I whispered back.

"Henry and I brought you presents."

Henry handed me a gift-wrapped package and so did Grace.

"Gosh," I said, sitting down on the couch between the kids, "I feel like it's my birthday or something. Which one should I open first?"

"Mine!" said Henry and Grace at the same time.

Everyone laughed. Then Mom asked Mr. and Mrs. Walker to sit down and she brought the lox and bagels out from the kitchen. While the adults ate, I tried to open both packages at the same time. I managed to do so by taking the ribbon off one, then the ribbon off the other, peeling the tape off one, then the tape off the other, and so on, until both presents were open.

Before me lay two pictures, one by Grace, one by Henry, only they had been professionally matted and framed.

"The framing is Mrs. Walker's and my gift to you," spoke up Mr. Walker.

"Thank you," I said. "I'll put these up in my new bedroom."

The Walkers stayed until the movers arrived, and then it was time to say good-bye. "Oh, I am going to miss you so much," I told Henry and Grace. "You, too," I said to their parents. Then we began hugging. (I cried, of course, and so did Grace, but only because she tripped over Henry's sneaker.)

The next couple of hours were chaos. The Walkers and the movers ran into each other in the hallway, and Grace tripped again. There was one moving company, but two moving vans — one for Dad, one for Mom and me. I was sure our stuff would get mixed up. (It didn't.)

All morning, the only words I heard were, "Van one," and "Van two," as the head mover told his men where to put our furniture and boxes.

Mom and Dad had three fights, all over matters I thought they'd already settled. The first was over who got the leather couch. (Mom won.) The second was over who got this pathetic old footstool that both my parents seem to love. (Dad won.) The third was over who got the cordless phone. (Mom won again. This was because Mom had also gotten the car, and to make up for it, Dad had gotten the microwave, the stereo, and two valuable paintings. But this did not seem like a fair trade, considering the poor condition of our station wagon. However, Mom and Dad didn't fight fair anymore, so I was the one who made the decision about the cordless phone.)

At long last, the vans and our car were loaded up. Laine had stayed for the whole morning, through the fights and everything. She was with us when Dad locked up our empty apartment, when we whizzed down to the lobby for the last time, when Dad handed our keys to Isaac, and when the vans pulled into the traffic. She waited (but stood at a discreet distance) while I said good-bye to Dad. Which, I might add, was one of the hardest things I have ever had to do.

Dad and I didn't cry, though. We'd already cried enough. We just held each other for a long time. Finally my father patted my back and said, "I'll see you in two weeks, honey." (I was going to visit him for the weekend.) Then he turned away from me, hailed a cab, called "Good-bye!" and was gone.

Mom climbed into our car.

Laine and I were left facing each other on the sidewalk.

"I'm not sure I made the right decision," I said.

"I am," Laine replied. "I saw your list."

I nodded. "I guess I'll see you in two weeks, too."

"Are you kidding? Of course you will. You

better see me every time you come to New York."

Laine sounded very cheerful, but her lower lip was trembling, so we just hugged quickly, and then I climbed into the car next to Mom.

" 'Bye, Mrs. McGill," said Laine.

" 'Bye, Laine," Mom replied.

We drove off.

Neither Mom nor I said a word until we'd left the city.

CHAPTER 14

The drive to Stoneybrook takes about two hours. It was at least an hour and a half before I began to feel even a smidge like a human again. For one thing, Mom said then, "Open my purse, Stacey. There's something in there for you from Laine."

"There is?" I replied. I reached into Mom's pocketbook and pulled out an envelope.

I held it for so long that Mom finally said, "Open it before I have an accident. I'm dying of curiosity!"

I opened it. Inside was half of a locket on a gold chain, and a note that said, "Dear Stace, I've got the other half. I'm wearing it now. Love, Laine." She must have been wearing it under her shirt, because I hadn't noticed it that morning. I put mine on under my shirt.

"I'll wear this every day," I told my mother.

Mom smiled. Then she said thoughtfully,

"Hmm. Today is Saturday. Just two days until your first meeting with the Baby-sitters Club."

"Yeah."

"And soon you'll get to visit Kristy's new sister again. You haven't seen Emily since the day they brought her home. I bet she's changed a lot."

"Yeah!" I said, remembering Kristy's photos.

"And your dad and I agreed that you can decorate your new room any way you want. Wallpaper, new bedspread, the works."

"Really? Thanks!"

By the time we reached Stoneybrook, I was so excited that I had butterflies in my stomach. I couldn't wait to get to our house, even though it wouldn't be our old house. Well, it would be *an* old house, but not *our* old house. I mean, not our former house. It would be our new old house.

What I was expecting to see when we pulled into the driveway were the moving vans, the big trees, the lawn, and the creaky old porch. What I wasn't expecting were all my friends and about half the kids in Stoneybrook. But there they were.

Claud, Mary Anne, Dawn, Jessi, Kristy, Mal, and Logan Bruno were standing in a bunch by the porch steps. Off to one side were Charlotte, all seven of Mallory's brothers and sisters, Kristy's brother David Michael, her stepbrother and stepsister (not little Emily, though), Jessi's sister, the Rodowsky boys, Gabbie and Myriah Perkins, Jamie Newton, the Arnold twins, Matt and Haley Braddock, and oh, I don't know who else. I was trying to look at everyone and scramble out of the car at the same time.

The little kids were holding a huge banner that read, WE KNEW YOU'D BE BACK, STACEY! And my friends were screaming, "Welcome back! Welcome home!"

I ran toward the members of the BSC with open arms. They ran toward me with open arms. We crashed into each other, laughing.

"Group hug!" cried Claudia.

And then the kids dropped their banner and ran to us baby-sitters. If you think there was hugging when I left New York, you should have seen what went on in the front yard of our new old house — although I have to admit that some of the boys, David Michael Thomas and Jackie Rodowsky in particular, said loudly that hugging was gross.

Then we were all distracted when Jackie, our walking disaster, fell over a packing carton and cut his lip. Mal took him through the backyards to her house to fix him up, and soon the kids began to drift home. At last, just Claudia, Kristy, Mary Anne, and Dawn remained. They watched the movers lug furniture and boxes into our house. After awhile, Mom took us all out for lunch. It was such a late lunch it was almost dinner. Then she dropped Kristy, Mary Anne, and Dawn off at their houses, but Claudia came home with me.

Same old Claud, I thought as we trudged up our front steps. Her hair was flowing down her back, pulled away from her face by a headband with a huge pink rose attached to it. She was wearing a long, oversized black-and-white sweater, skin-tight black leggings, pink-and-black socks, and black ballet slippers. Her jewelry was new, and I could tell she'd made it herself. You know those things about a best friend. Her necklace was a string of glazed beads that she'd probably made in her pottery class. And from her ears dangled an alarming number of plastic charms attached to gold hoops.

"Where's your room?" Claudia asked.

"First one on the left, upstairs," I told her. "Let's see if the movers got all my stuff into it."

They hadn't.

"Mo-om!" I yelled downstairs. "The movers put my bed in your room and your bed in my room."

"You're kidding!" replied Mom. She ran upstairs to take a look. "Yup, you're right," she said.

"Now what?" I asked. If this had happened in New York, Dad and the super would have grunted and huffed, taken the beds apart, and switched them around. Instead, Mom and Claud and I grunted and huffed, took the beds apart, and switched them around. It wasn't easy, but we did it.

"Women can do anything," Mom remarked proudly.

"Except be fathers," I pointed out.

No one knew whether to cry or laugh. Finally we laughed. I hadn't meant to be mean.

"Anyway," said Claudia, "I think mothers *can* be fathers and fathers *can* be mothers — sort of. Look at Mr. Spier. He's Mary Anne's father *and* mother. Mary Anne has always said so, and I think she's right."

Mom kissed the top of Claud's head. "Thank you. I'm glad to see that Stacey has such a sensible friend," she said. "Now I'm going to leave you to your unpacking. I'll see you later." Mom left the room.

"Wow," exclaimed Claud. "No one has ever described me as sensible."

"You have to be sensible to be a good baby-sitter," I pointed out.

"Yeah, but my parents and teachers mostly describe me as outlandish or wild."

"Doesn't apply herself," I added, mimicking this math teacher Claud had in seventh grade.

"Doesn't concentrate," said Claudia.

But then I said, "Artistic, kind, understanding, funny, good with children, and smarter than most people think she is."

Claud looked at me gratefully. Then the two of us surveyed my room. It was a mess. The movers had put the furniture where they'd thought I'd want it, but they'd thought wrong. And against one wall was a huge stack of boxes.

"Where do we begin?" asked Claudia, who has never moved in her life.

"With my clothes," I replied, giggling.

Claud laughed, too. "Boy, is it good to have you back." She paused. Then she said slowly, "You know, when Mimi died, I thought *my* life was over, too. I really did. I missed you more then than at any other time. You couldn't have filled the empty spot Mimi left in my soul, but you would have made me feel better."

"Did it help that I came for the funeral?" I asked. Claud and I were opening my suitcases. I tried to remember where I'd packed the coat hangers.

"Oh, yes!" cried Claud. "Are you kidding? Even though we couldn't be together during the funeral, I was aware that you were there. The whole time. I really was. You kept me from going crazy."

Claudia and I both stopped working for a moment and I knew we were remembering that sunny day when we'd buried Mimi, watching whatever was left of her as she was lowered into a cold hole in the ground. Claudia had tossed a flower onto her casket.

Claud sighed.

I sighed. No matter how glad Claudia was that I'd returned, no matter how good the timing was, Mimi-wise, I still wasn't one hundred percent happy about being back in Stoneybrook. So I said to Claud what I'd said to Laine that morning: "I'm not sure I made the right decision."

"About what?" Claudia looked up from an open suitcase. I'd found the hangers and was carefully arranging my clothes in the closet as Claud unpacked them and handed them to me.

"About — about — " I floundered. I didn't want Claud to think I wasn't glad to be with her again, but . . . but I wasn't. Not entirely. "About which of my parents to live with," I said finally.

"You had to choose one of them," said Claud matter-of-factly.

"I know, but then the other one was hurt and it's my fault."

"No, it isn't. *You* didn't ask for this divorce. *They* wanted it. Parents can do things their kids don't have any control over at all."

"Yeah," I replied thoughtfully. "Sometimes I understand it because, after all, they *are* the adults. Other times it doesn't seem fair. But then I think, They're feeding us, they're taking care of us. You know."

"I'm not sure that gives them the right to do whatever they want to us, though," said Claud. "Look how unhappy they've made you."

"Do I actually *look* unhappy?" I asked.

"Not as unhappy as I'd expected. I thought you'd be crying your eyes out."

"Oh, believe me. I already have. There aren't any tears left."

"Well, I just want you to know," said Claud, handing me a shirt, "that I understand if you aren't completely happy to be back."

"You do?"

"Sure. *I* love Stoneybrook, but I grew up here. You grew up in great big, glamorous New York City. And you had to leave your dad behind."

I didn't know what to say. I guess I should have given Claudia more credit — I mean, for understanding. That's what best friends are for. And Claud is my Connecticut best friend.

Finally I just said, "Thank you," which didn't quite follow Claud's statement, but I knew she knew what I meant.

Then I changed the subject. "Mom said I could decorate my room any way I want. You know, new rug, curtains, wallpaper, whatever."

"Wow! Can I help?"

This project was right up Claudia's alley.

"You better," I told her. "I'll need your opinions."

"What colors are you thinking of?"

"Blue and white," I replied immediately.

"Your stuff's already blue and white."

"Well, I want *different* blue and white stuff."

Claudia laughed. "I am *so* glad you're back!" she cried. She held her arms out and we hugged.

But I could not say, "I'm glad to be back." Not then, anyway.

CHAPTER 15

Mom and I didn't finish unpacking until almost a week later. When we did finish, the house still looked awfully bare.

"Well, we *did* move just half an apartment full of stuff into a whole huge house," said Mom.

I burst out laughing.

"What?" asked my mother.

"The yard sale!" I hooted. "Don't you remember the yard sale?"

When we were moving *away* from Stoneybrook at the beginning of the school year, we had decided that we could never fit all the stuff we'd bought to fill up our house into our new apartment in the city. So we'd held a yard sale and gotten rid of some of it.

"Maybe we could buy it back," said Mom, with a grin.

"Yeah! For the same price we sold it — twenty-dollar couches, that sort of thing."

"Actually," said Mom, "you've got a point. We could buy things at other people's yard sales. We'll never have enough money for all new furniture."

"Are you sure we can afford to decorate my room?"

"I'm positive. That's special. Your dad and I talked it over and set aside money for it. You can fix up your room in New York, too."

This all sounded kind of like a pay-off — for letting my parents get a divorce. But of course I couldn't say that.

"So how's school?" asked Mom. It was Friday afternoon. I had been back at Stoneybrook Middle School for five days. I had to admit that I felt as if I'd never been away. I hadn't been lying when I'd written on my list of New York versus Stoneybrook that I liked SMS better than my private school in New York. The kids in Stoneybrook are just as cliquey as the ones in the city, but they aren't nearly as snobby. I'm not saying that *all* kids who go to private schools are snobs (because then I'd be calling myself a snob!), but that an awful lot of the ones at my old school were snobs.

"School's great," I admitted to Mom.

"And math?"

I'm an excellent math student, and when I'd returned to SMS, the teachers had put me into the high-school level algebra class. It was hard — but fun.

"Math is fine. It's — it's no problem. Get it?" I said. "No *problem?*"

Mom just shook her head.

"Well, I better go," I said. "I'm sitting for Charlotte this afternoon, and then I have a meeting of the Baby-sitters Club. I'll be home a little after six, okay?"

"Okay."

I put on my jacket and headed for the door.

I opened the door.

I waited.

" 'Bye!" I called.

" 'Bye!" said Mom.

I waited again.

Nothing.

Mom had not said, "Have fun and be careful," once since we'd re-arrived in Stoneybrook. I kind of missed it.

I climbed onto my ten-speed and headed for Charlotte's. When I reached her house, I chained my bike to the Johanssens' lamppost

(I probably didn't need to, but New York habits die hard), and ran to their front door. Charlotte opened it before I rang the bell.

"Stacey! Stacey! Stacey!" she cried.

It was my first official sitting job for Charlotte since my return, and we were both pretty excited.

"Hi, Dr. Johanssen," I greeted Charlotte's mother.

"Oh, Stacey, is it ever good to have you back," she replied.

Dr. Johanssen and I like each other a lot. She helped me through a bad time with my diabetes right after our first move to Stoneybrook.

"Stacey, I have to show you something!" Charlotte cried, and flew up to her room to get whatever it was.

"I think you're going to find a new Charlotte," said Dr. Johanssen in a low tone, as she put on her coat. She smiled at me. "She's more outgoing, she's happier, and she even has a few friends now — but she still needs you." Dr. Johanssen paused at the bottom of the stairs. "I'm leaving now, Charlotte," she called. "I'll be at the hospital. Daddy will be home by five-fifteen. You and Stacey know where the emergency numbers are."

"Okay, Mom!" replied Charlotte. She didn't even come out of her room.

Dr. Johanssen raised her eyebrows as if to say, "You see how she's changed?" The old Charlotte would have run downstairs to give her mother a desperate good-bye kiss.

Dr. J. was right. Charlotte and I had fun that afternoon, and Charlotte was still sweet and thoughtful and more interested in reading books than in doing anything else. But she was no longer clingy and frightened. And she got three phone calls from friends, and chatted away with them.

Charlotte was growing up.

Mr. J. came home promptly at five-fifteen, and I jumped on my bike and headed over to Claudia's for the BSC meeting. It was my third since I'd returned to Stoneybrook, and I have to say that I relished every minute of each one.

I was the first to arrive at the Kishis', so I settled myself in my usual spot on Claudia's bed and watched her conduct a search for junk food. She was a little low that day and found only a roll of Lifesavers, a pack of those Twinkies with that disgusting fruit-and-creme mixture inside of them, and a bag of taco chips.

Then I got to watch the other members arrive. Kristy thundered up the stairs in her jeans, sneakers, a sweater, and a turtleneck. Mary Anne entered Claud's room quietly, wearing a new flared green dress. Dawn bounced into the room in a pair of jeans with zippers up the legs, her long hair flowing down her back like a blonde waterfall. Jessi ran in breathlessly, straight from a dance class, her leotard still on under her clothes. And Mal arrived last, wearing a totally new outfit — a sequined sweat shirt, a short skirt, and pink leggings. None of us had seen her dressed like that before. Apparently, her mother and father hadn't, either.

"Can you believe it?" exclaimed Mal, without even saying hi to us. "My parents practically had nervous breakdowns over these clothes. I bought them with my own money, which I'm allowed to do, but they say this outfit's too grown up. I'm *eleven*, for heaven's sake."

This is an old Mallory problem. We've heard the story before, but it doesn't mean we don't sympathize with Mal, so we listened patiently while she went on. (Luckily for Mal, it was only 5:25, so she had five minutes to talk before Kristy would get antsy.)

"What do they *want?*" wailed Mal. "I've

stopped asking to get contact lenses. And I got the stupid braces they're making me wear for two years. Sheesh."

"Mal," I began, but she didn't hear me.

"I wish," she said at last, "that I could do something really great to prove to Mom and Dad that I'm not just a kid anymore."

Kristy, Dawn, Mary Anne, Claudia, and I looked at each other. Sometimes Mal seems *so* young. But we made a few suggestions to her, and then Kristy began itching to bring the meeting to order. So she did.

"Any club business?" she asked.

The rest of us shook our heads. I was glad it was a Friday. If it had been a Monday, I would have had to collect our club dues, and nobody likes to part with her money.

Yes, that's right. Dawn had gratefully given me my old job of treasurer back. She's not as good at math as I am, and she'd liked being an alternate officer.

"More variety," she'd said. "I get to try all the offices. I just wish you guys would be absent more often so I could fill in for you. Kristy, I don't think you've *ever* missed a meeting. I'm dying to be president for a day."

"Not a chance," said Kristy, grinning.

The phone rang then. Kristy and Dawn dove

for it, but Dawn reached it first. "Hello, Baby-sitters Club," she said. "Oh, hi, Mrs. Perkins. . . . Tuesday afternoon? We'll check and get right back to you." Dawn hung up and announced that Mrs. Perkins needed a sitter for Myriah, Gabbie, and Laura on the following Tuesday. Kristy got the job, and Dawn called Mrs. Perkins to tell her so.

By six o'clock, the meeting ended, we'd lined up five jobs and eaten the whole bag of taco chips.

Mal and I rode our bikes home together.

"Are you glad you're back?" Mal asked as we approached my turn-off.

"Yes," I told her. But deep down I knew that I would never — *ever* — stop missing Dad or wishing that my parents were still together. But those were my private thoughts and I knew I was lucky. Lucky that my parents would let me go back and forth between them as long as it didn't affect my schoolwork, lucky that I didn't have to listen to fights anymore, lucky that since my mom insisted on moving she'd at least decided to return to Stoney-brook, where I could be with my old BSC friends.

"Yes," I said again to Mallory. "I'm glad I'm back."

Mal smiled. "I'll call you tomorrow. Maybe I could come over now that we're neighbors."

"Definitely." I returned Mal's smile.

Then I rode down the street to Mom and my new home.

Dear Reader,

In *Welcome Back, Stacey*, Stacey has been away from Stoneybrook since book #13. During the time that she was away, I realized that she was a crucial member of the Baby-sitters Club, and I wanted to return her to Stoneybrook. Also during that time, I was beginning to receive more and more letters. Many of them were from readers whose parents were going through a divorce, just like Stacey's. Some of them, like Stacey, were faced with difficult decisions. They said that they felt confused, and wished they could read a story about a favorite character who is in their position. And that was how the idea for *Welcome Back, Stacey* was born.

Happy reading,

Ann M. Martin

L. GODWIN

Ann M. Martin

About the Author

ANN MATTHEWS MARTIN was born on August 12, 1955. She grew up in Princeton, NJ, with her parents and her younger sister, Jane.

Although Ann used to be a teacher and then an editor of children's books, she's now a full-time writer. She gets the ideas for her books from many different places. Some are based on personal experiences. Others are based on childhood memories and feelings. Many are written about contemporary problems or events.

All of Ann's characters, even the members of the Baby-sitters Club, are made up. (So is Stoneybrook.) But many of her characters are based on real people. Sometimes Ann names her characters after people she knows, other times she chooses names she likes.

In addition to the Baby-sitters Club books, Ann Martin has written many other books for children. Her favorite is *Ten Kids, No Pets* because she loves big families and she loves animals. Her favorite Baby-sitters Club book is *Kristy's Big Day*. (By the way, Kristy is her favorite baby-sitter!)

Ann M. Martin now lives in New York with her cats, Gussie and Woody. Her hobbies are reading, sewing, and needlework — especially making clothes for children.

Notebook Pages

This Baby-sitters Club book belongs to _____ .

I am _____ years old and in the _____

grade.

The name of my school is _____ .

I got this BSC book from _____ .

I started reading it on _____ and

finished reading it on _____ .

The place where I read most of this book is _____ .

My favorite part was when _____ .

If I could change anything in the story, it might be the part when

_____ .

My favorite character in the Baby-sitters Club is _____ .

The BSC member I am most like is _____

because _____ .

If I could write a Baby-sitters Club book it would be about ____

_____ .

#28 Welcome Back, Stacey!

In *Welcome Back, Stacey!*, Stacey decides to move back to Stoney-brook. If I had to choose between living in Stoneybrook or living in New York City, I would choose to live in _____ _____ because _____ _____ .

Stacey's friends in the Baby-sitters Club are thrilled when she moves back to Stoneybrook. If anyone could move to my town, I would want it to be _____ .

Right now, this person lives in _____ .

When Stacey comes home to Stoneybrook, the BSC members make her a big welcome back banner. If I were to make a welcome back banner for one of my friends, it would look like this:

Here I am, age three.

Me with Charlot
my "almos

A family portrait — me
with my parents.

SCRAP BOOK

hanssen,
ster."

Getting ready for school.

In LUV at Shadow Lake.

Read all the books
about **Stacey**
in the Baby-sitters Club series
by Ann M. Martin

THE BABY-SITTERS CLUB®

The best friends you'll ever have!

Collect 'em all!

by Ann M. Martin

More titles... ▶

The Baby-sitters Club titles continued...

❏ MG48222-X	#78	**Claudia and the Crazy Peaches**	**$3.50**
❏ MG48223-8	#79	**Mary Anne Breaks the Rules**	**$3.50**
❏ MG48224-6	#80	**Mallory Pike, #1 Fan**	**$3.50**
❏ MG48225-4	#81	**Kristy and Mr. Mom**	**$3.50**
❏ MG48226-2	#82	**Jessi and the Troublemaker**	**$3.50**
❏ MG48235-1	#83	**Stacey vs. the BSC**	**$3.50**
❏ MG48228-9	#84	**Dawn and the School Spirit War**	**$3.50**
❏ MG48236-X	#85	**Claudi Kishli, Live from WSTO**	**$3.50**
❏ MG48227-0	#86	**Mary Anne and Camp BSC**	**$3.50**
❏ MG48237-8	#87	**Stacey and the Bad Girls**	**$3.50**
❏ MG22872-2	#88	**Farewell, Dawn**	**$3.50**
❏ MG22873-0	#89	**Kristy and the Dirty Diapers**	**$3.50**
❏ MG22874-9	#90	**Welcome to the BSC, Abby**	**$3.50**
❏ MG22875-1	#91	**Claudia and the First Thanksgiving**	**$3.50**
❏ MG22876-5	#92	**Mallory's Christmas Wish**	**$3.50**
❏ MG22877-3	#93	**Mary Anne and the Memory Garden**	**$3.99**
❏ MG22878-1	#94	**Stacey McGill, Super Sitter**	**$3.99**
❏ MG45575-3		**Logan's Story Special Edition Readers' Request**	**$3.25**
❏ MG47118-X		**Logan Bruno, Boy Baby-sitter**	
		Special Edition Readers' Request	**$3.50**
❏ MG47756-0		**Shannon's Story Special Edition**	**$3.50**
❏ MG47686-6		**The Baby-sitters Club Guide to Baby-sitting**	**$3.25**
❏ MG47314-X		**The Baby-sitters Club Trivia and Puzzle Fun Book**	**$2.50**
❏ MG48400-1		**BSC Portrait Collection: Claudia's Book**	**$3.50**
❏ MG22864-1		**BSC Portrait Collection: Dawn's Book**	**$3.50**
❏ MG48399-4		**BSC Portrait Collection: Stacey's Book**	**$3.50**
❏ MG47151-1		**The Baby-sitters Club Chain Letter**	**$14.95**
❏ MG48295-5		**The Baby-sitters Club Secret Santa**	**$14.95**
❏ MG45074-3		**The Baby-sitters Club Notebook**	**$2.50**
❏ MG44783-1		**The Baby-sitters Club Postcard Book**	**$4.95**

Available wherever you buy books...or use this order form.

Scholastic Inc., P.O. Box 7502, 2931 E. McCarty Street, Jefferson City, MO 65102

Please send me the books I have checked above. I am enclosing $_____
(please add $2.00 to cover shipping and handling). Send check or money order–no cash or
C.O.D.s please.

Name _____ Birthdate_____

Address _____

City_____ State/Zip _____

Please allow four to six weeks for delivery. Offer good in the U.S. only. Sorry, mail orders are not available
to residents of Canada. Prices subject to change.